For you, who love birds.

"An egg is always an adventure…"
— Oscar Wilde

"I think that, if required on pain of death to name instantly the most perfect thing in the universe, I should risk my fate on a bird's egg."
— Thomas Wentworth Higginson

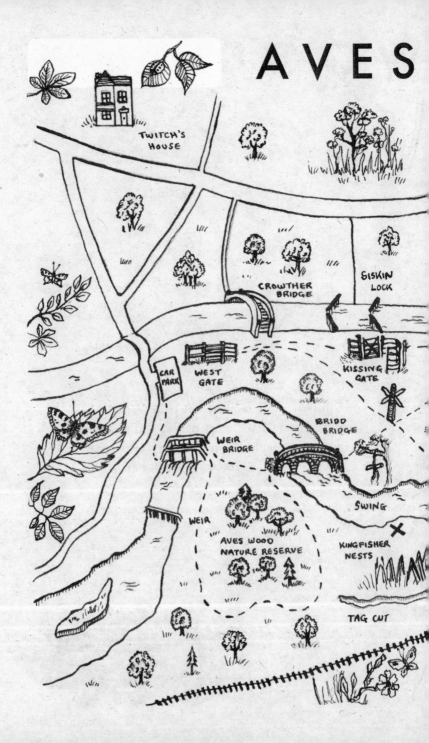

PRAISE FOR *TWITCH*

"Leonard knows her audience and the jeopardy comes in flocks… Find your nest, curl up and enjoy."
THE TIMES, CHILDREN'S BOOK OF THE WEEK

"A twist-laden, thriller-like tale."
OBSERVER

"A lively, twisty crime drama as well as a persuasive story about friendship and protecting nature."
SUNDAY TIMES

"Another soaring success from Leonard."
DAILY MAIL

"A tale of friendship, of being yourself, of seeking solace in nature … simply genius."
BBC WILDLIFE

"[A] pacy mystery adventure."
iNEWSPAPER

"A superb adventure of friendship, bravery and the wonderful world of birds."
THE BOOKSELLER

"One of those really, really good books!"
THE BOOKBAG

95100000404923

"A winged masterpiece."
MAZ EVANS

"Enthralling from beginning to end, it really touched my young bird-loving heart!"
DARA McANULTY

"Glorious! Full of excitement and wonder!"
SOPHIE ANDERSON

"Brave and thrilling."
JASBINDER BILAN

"Birds, mystery and fowl play! What more could you want?"
GILL LEWIS

"Cracking characters, beyond pacy plotting and an ending that is almost Bugsy Malone-esque!"
PHIL EARLE

"A delight from start to finish."
ABI ELPHINSTONE

"An absolute triumph."
CHRISTOPHER EDGE

"*Twitch* is a compelling read… An adventure mystery with birds – what more could any reader want?!"
STEPHEN MOSS

"Adventure, friendship and the pure unassuming beauty of nature … a book that could have been a collaboration between David Attenborough and Roald Dahl."
DR JESS FRENCH

"Delightful and marvellous."
LIZ HYDER

"WILDly good!"
MATT OLDFIELD

CLUTCH

M. G. LEONARD

WALKER
BOOKS

First published 2023 by Walker Books Ltd
87 Vauxhall Walk, London SE11 5HJ

2 4 6 8 10 9 7 5 3 1

Text © 2023 MG Leonard Ltd.
Cover illustrations © 2023 Paddy Donnelly
Map illustrations © 2021, 2022 and 2023 Laurissa Jones

The right of M. G. Leonard to be identified as author of
this work has been asserted in accordance with
the Copyright, Designs and Patents Act 1988

This book has been typeset in Berkeley and Futura

Printed and bound by CPI Group (UK) Ltd, Croydon CR0 4YY

British Library Cataloguing in Publication Data:
a catalogue record for this book is available from the British Library

ISBN 978-1-5295-0610-5

www.walker.co.uk

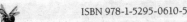

MIX
Paper | Supporting
responsible forestry
FSC® C171272

WOOD

BRIDDVALE ROAD

THE FISHING LAKE

CAR PARK

AVES LOCK

CANAL

EAST GATE

TWITCH'S HIDE

POND

RAILWAY LINE

1

POACHED!

Twitch winced as a needle-sharp spike raked the back of his hand. The pale graze turned red as his blood sought to knit his skin back together. He ignored it. He had to see what was going on. Why were there two police cars at the bottom of Passerine Pike?

"Please don't let it be the peregrine falcons," he whispered to himself, as a creeping dread drove him up the barbed hawthorn tree. "Please." He felt a sob building in the base of his throat as he spotted torch beams bumbling about at the top of the hill. That was where the nest was. He swallowed the marble of emotion, forcing himself up the bunch-backed tree, his heart hopping anxiously.

Since he and his best friend, Jack, had witnessed the death-defying aerial display of the courting falcons in late February, they had regularly trekked up Passerine Pike to watch the birds. Twitch remembered the male bird rocketing skywards, spiralling up until it was a speck, then plunging down at a speed that had stopped his breath. It had pulled out of its dive at the very last moment, rolling, climbing, looping the loop. The female falcon had swooped in, locking talons with the male. They seemed to tumble out of control: whirling, falling, spinning, rising.

Jack had thought the birds were fighting.

Laughing, Twitch had explained that they were kind of kissing.

The peregrine falcons had built a nest, an eyrie, on a high ledge of one of the ancient rocks protruding from the top of the hill like giant's teeth.

The highest bough of the hawthorn tree, which grew out of the hedgerow that marked the border between public land and the private Mord Estate, was the only place from which you could see into the nest without upsetting the birds. Through their binoculars, Twitch and Jack had spotted a clutch of perfect rust-brown speckled eggs and celebrated with a silent high five.

The fear that something might have happened to the falcons was making Twitch feel sick. Reaching up, leaning back, he lifted his bottom into the highest junction of hawthorn branches, wedging himself safely in the arms of the tree. Yanking out his binoculars, he ran his finger over the focusing dial. The blur became a nest, but he saw no birds. He felt as if he had been punched in the stomach by Vernon, the biggest boy in his class. The nest was empty! He looked up, desperately searching the pewter sky for the falcons. Where could they be? Had they abandoned their nest? Had they been hurt?

Looking back through his binoculars, Twitch counted three police officers searching the ground around the rocks and one in a climbing harness up near the nest. He spied the familiar, clean-shaven face of Constable Greenwood, who was frowning, holding his chin as he listened to a female officer who Twitch had never seen before. Concentrating on her lips, Twitch tried to read what the officer was saying.

Jack could read lips because his older brother, David, was deaf. Jack had taught all his friends sign language, but Twitch had wanted to learn how to lip-read too. It was a useful way of silently communicating when watching birds or mouthing a secret message at school.

Focusing on the female officer's mouth, Twitch missed some words but then clearly made out two: *egg thief*.

It was as if his insides had been doused with icy water. Instantly he understood what had happened. Shoving his binoculars into his coat pocket, Twitch scrambled down the tree, barely noticing the thorns.

An egg thief! In Briddvale! This was disastrous for all birds. It was spring! Nesting season! He needed to get to Jack, immediately.

Landing clumsily, he staggered then ran, hurtling down the hill. His long brackish-blond fringe flew back from his face as the biting chill of the evening air caught at his throat. He sprinted into the car park, an empty disco of spinning blue lights, passing a silver VW Golf. He glimpsed a gaunt young man with a shaved head in the driver's seat, staring up at the drama on the hill. When he reached the end of the lane, he heard a girl call his name. Glancing over his shoulder, he saw nine-year-old Pippa Bettany, the granddaughter of the Briddvale newsagent, Twitch's boss. She waved. He raised a hand in reply but ran on.

Once on tarmac, Twitch regulated his stride, falling into a rhythm, pulling his knees up, throwing his fists forward, breathing in through his nose and out through his mouth. He flew past naked trees, knobbly with new buds. He barely noticed passing Patchem's farm. Slowing to cross Briddvale Road, he sped up again over the canal, turning onto the footpath, his feet thudding on the compact earth; finally, he entered the alley that wove along the back of the houses on Redshank Road. He stopped in front of a tall garden gate, gulping down lungfuls of air. His head throbbed as if a woodpecker were hammering at his temples. He leaned on the fence post, closing his eyes as he caught his breath. His mind showed him the image of the empty nest. His eyelids sprang open. He turned the ring handle, lifting the latch, and let himself into a manicured garden.

It was dark now. Night had fallen whilst he'd been running.

Through the glass doors at the back of the house, he could see Jack's mum and dad, sitting at their kitchen table. They were chatting, smiling, holding glasses of red wine, surrounded by the scattered plates of a recently eaten dinner. Twitch suddenly felt like he was intruding. He was about to sneak over to the side gate and go round to the front door when the bathroom light flickered on upstairs. He instantly recognized Jack's silhouette. The window was ajar. Taking out his phone and turning up the volume, Twitch stood beneath the window. He hit play on a track he'd labelled "Spark Bird" and his phone emitted the eerie cry of a nightjar. It was a high gurgling sound, like a singing chorus of strangled frogs. The nightjar was the bird that had sparked Twitch's passion for birdwatching. Jack knew this.

The window opened wide. Jack's head popped out. "Twitch?"

"Jack!" Twitch hissed, waving his hands. "Down here."

"What are you doing here?" Jack looked amazed to see him. "I thought we were meeting in the morning after your paper round?"

"Something terrible has happened..." Twitch felt his chest clench and he couldn't go on. In his race to get here, he hadn't let himself think about the falcons. Jack had been so excited to see their fluffy chicks hatch and fledge.

"Climb up the trellis," Jack said, seeing Twitch was upset. "It'll hold. I've done it loads."

Focusing on the footholds and handholds needed to scale the wall, Twitch climbed until he felt Jack's hands grabbing his shoulders and hauling him in through the bathroom window. The pair of them fell to the linoleum floor. Jack laughed as he sat up. Seeing Twitch's face, he stopped.

"What is it? What's wrong?"

"Oh, Jack!" Twitch exclaimed. "They're gone!"

"Who are?"

"The peregrine falcons." Twitch stared at his best friend's uncomprehending face. "Their nest is empty."

"Empty?" Jack frowned. "But what about the eggs ... their babies?"

"They've been taken" – Twitch shook his head – "by an egg thief!"

2

BOYS OF A FEATHER

Twitch watched Jack take in the awful news. His friend pushed his fingers through his upright caramel fringe, repeating Twitch's words.

"Taken by an egg thief?" Jack paused. "Do you mean by another animal, a predator … to eat or something?"

"No." Twitch's shoulders slumped. He suddenly felt exhausted. "Falcons know how to defend their nests against predators. That's why they build them high, on rocks, so they're difficult to reach." He shook his head. "A human took them. The police are up at Passerine Pike right now, investigating."

"What?" Jack rose to his knees, banging his head on the underside of the sink. "Ow!" He didn't take his eyes from Twitch as he rubbed his bump. "But why? What kind of a person steals birds' eggs?"

"Egg collectors do."

"Egg collectors!" Jack echoed. "People don't really do that, do they? That's like … kidnapping baby birds from their families."

"It's worse." Twitch's voice was a rasp. "It's murder."

"Murder!"

"Egg collectors only care about the shell. They blow the eggs to get rid of the growing bird inside."

Jack's top lip curled in disgust.

"A peregrine falcon's nest is its home." Grief rose like a wave inside Twitch. "They return to it every spring. But, if they're still alive, our falcons will never return to Passerine Pike." He tried to blink back his tears, but several escaped down his cheeks. "And they won't produce another clutch of eggs this year."

"We need to find their eggs, quickly, and put them back." Jack got to his feet.

"It's too late. Unless the eggs are in an incubator, the chicks will already be dead."

There was a horrible silence as the boys thought about the baby peregrine falcons that would never hatch. Jack's eyes were glassy with tears.

Anger, like slow-burning coals, glowed white-hot in the pit of Twitch's stomach. "There are barely fifteen hundred nesting pairs of peregrine falcons in the whole country." He clenched his fists. "They're on the brink of extinction. A clutch of baby peregrine falcons is precious."

"Scumbag!" Jack exclaimed suddenly, throwing a punch at the shower curtain hanging over the bath. It swished aside. "We can't let them get away with this." He yanked open the door. "Come on. We're going to find out who stole those eggs and stop them from ever doing it again."

Twitch got up. This was why he'd come. Jack was an excellent detective who loved the challenge of a difficult case. He and Twitch were part of a crime-solving, birdwatching club called the Twitchers. They had already solved two dangerous crimes. Tomorrow was the start of the Easter holidays. At school, that afternoon, Ozuru, Terry, Jack and Twitch had all cheered when Tara had announced that Ava and Tippi were coming to visit, arriving in Briddvale by train the next morning. The Twitchers would be together again. It had been months since the seven of them had gathered at the hide in Aves Wood. Twitch had been planning to bring everyone to see the falcons' nest, which is why he'd gone to Passerine Pike this evening, to check on the birds. Now, instead, the Twitchers would be solving the mystery of who had stolen their eggs.

"How are we going to stop the egg thief?" Twitch

asked, following Jack across the landing and into his bedroom.

"I don't know yet, but the police won't have the resources to stop someone committing crimes against birds. They'll only be able to act if there's a witness. Remember how stretched they were last year when those cats were being shot at? And they were pets!"

"It's up to us." Twitch felt a surge of determination.

"Exactly." Jack grabbed a notebook and pen from the desk next to his bed.

Twitch perched on the stool for Jack's drum kit. On the wall above him hung a photograph he'd taken last October of a bearded vulture, a lammergeier. He and Jack had seen the rare bird together. That moment had cemented their friendship for ever.

"The case of the egg thief," Jack pronounced dramatically, dropping onto his bed. "Tara found this book for me in the library about solving crimes. I've been reading it. It's so good. It mentions this thing called profiling. We should try it."

"Profiling?"

"You gather all the facts you can about a crime. Then you deduce what kind of a person is likely to have committed it. When you're considering suspects, you focus on the people that match your profile."

"We don't have any suspects."

"Not yet," Jack agreed, rolling onto his stomach. He took the lid off his pen. "Let's start with the geography of the crime: where it took place."

"The eggs were stolen from the nest at the top of the pike."

"Which is outdoors, on public land. Anyone up there is visible from miles around. It's the highest hill in Briddvale. People climb it all the time."

"You'd have to be really lucky not to be spotted climbing up to the nest to steal the eggs in daylight."

"Which is why the thief must've taken them at night," Jack deduced.

"If I were the thief" – Twitch tried to imagine taking the eggs – "I'd scope out the nest in the daylight, then go back when it was dark, and no one was around."

"Yes!" Jack scribbled something down. "Which means the eggs must have been stolen last night or very early this morning."

"I was at the pike yesterday at about six-thirty. The eggs were fine. The female falcon was sitting on them."

"You went last night?" Jack looked up, surprised. "But we checked on the birds before school."

"I know." Twitch felt himself flush. "They hunt at dusk. I wanted to watch."

"Did you see anyone up there?"

Twitch thought back to the previous evening. "There was a man, a stranger. He wasn't up near the peak though. He was walking along the path above the car park. I don't think he's local."

"Suspect number one," Jack said, scribbling in the notebook. "We need to find out who he is. He might have been waiting for you to leave, so he could pinch the eggs. What did he look like?"

"Tall, lanky. He was wearing one of those khaki waistcoats with lots of pockets on the front. He had on an olive-green cap, and a tatty rucksack with a fishing rod strapped to the side."

"Those waistcoat pockets would be useful for storing stolen eggs."

"He was behaving weirdly," Twitch remembered. "Walking slowly, bent down, staring at the ground."

"Perhaps he'd dropped something," Jack suggested. "Or maybe he was trying to hide his face."

Twitch shook his head. The man hadn't looked like he was trying to hide.

"Did you see anyone else?" Jack asked. "Or anything out of the ordinary?"

"Not that I remember."

"What about tonight? Tell me what you saw."

"There are four police officers on the pike. One was using climbing gear to get up to the nest. Constable Greenwood was talking to a female officer. I read her lips. That's how I know they think it's an egg thief."

"Nice work!" Jack looked impressed.

"Pippa called to me as I ran out of the car park," Twitch remembered.

"Pippa Bettany?" Jack's tone was scornful. "Is that little kid still following you around?"

"Yeah." Twitch rolled his eyes. "Every time she sees me, she launches into a monologue about birds. I never know what to say. Luckily, this time, I was already running away."

"I swear she was stalking you the other day." Jack chuckled. "When we were walking by the canal."

"Every time I look over my shoulder, she's there."

"Someone's got a crush…" Jack said in a singsong voice.

"I have not!"

"I meant her, you idiot."

"Oh! Right."

"Let's get back to our profile." Jack looked down at his notebook. "What does the scene of the crime tell us about the criminal? The nest is on a high rock up a big hill, so it's unlikely our thief is old. Or if they are, they must be super fit. Anyone injured or frightened of heights couldn't climb up to the nest."

"If the thief climbed the pike at night," Twitch said, "it's unlikely they're a child. Most children would be at home, in bed."

"Unless they're working with an adult…" Jack tapped his pen against his teeth, then shrugged. "But, yeah, probably not a kid." He paused. "The thief would need equipment … torches, rock-climbing gear, that sort of thing."

"That's what I was thinking."

"OK, so if I'm an egg thief" – Jack closed his eyes – "what kind of person am I?"

"Secretive," Twitch replied instantly.

Jack's eyes sprang open. "Why?"

"Collecting eggs is illegal. That's why the police were up at Passerine Pike. If you are caught with a collection of wild birds' eggs, you can be sent to prison."

Jack looked astonished. "But I've seen egg collections in museums."

"Some of the eggs you see in museums aren't real. My grandad knew this artist over in Thrushcombe who makes replica eggs for museums and galleries out of plaster and resin. What was his name…? Peter something…" Twitch screwed up his face as he tried to remember. "Peter Landrow. That's it. He paints fake eggs to make them look real. We've got one on our living-room mantelpiece. The guillemot's egg. He gave it to me at Grandad's funeral."

"You've shown it to me." Jack nodded.

"My grandad and Mr Landrow grew up together. When they were kids, they collected birds' eggs."

"What!" Jack was aghast. "Your grandad!"

"It wasn't illegal back then because there were lots of birds. Only when people realized bird populations were shrinking did they make egg collecting a crime. Grandad told me that eggers – that's what egg collectors call themselves, or, if they're being posh, oologists—"

"Oologists!"

"Yeah! Anyway, Grandad said that eggers who loved their collections couldn't stop. Obsessed collectors kept doing it. They're addicted."

"Weird thing to be addicted to."

"That's why the authorities had to make owning an egg collection a crime. Places like museums are allowed to have old collections, but that's it."

"So, if I were an egger, I'd have to hide my collection?"

Twitch nodded. "You couldn't tell your friends or family in case someone dobbed you in to the police.

They would take your collection away and you'd go to prison."

"An egger must collect all kinds of eggs, which means I'm probably good at climbing trees." He wrote this down. "I must be fit and outdoorsy, probably between the ages of eighteen and fifty-five-ish. I'm a loner, with secrets, and addicted to collecting." Jack thought for a moment. "Unless … can you sell rare eggs? I mean, are they worth money? Could someone be stealing the eggs to sell to rich oologists?"

"I don't know." Twitch frowned. "I mean, it's possible, but you'd have to be paid a lot of money to risk going to prison for an egg. I think the thief is probably stealing for their own collection." He considered the picture of the person Jack was creating. "And they must know a lot about birds. Nests can be hard to find. You'd need to know about habitats, times of year for laying, the number of eggs in a clutch, their size, what they look like. The thief has to be a birdwatcher!"

"Imagine watching birds so you can kidnap their babies!" Jack looked disgusted. "That's dark!" He shook his head. "My first thought was that this might be the kind of thing that Richard Peak or Tom Madden would do for money…"

"No." Twitch had already ruled out the two teenagers

who'd mercilessly bullied Jack last year. "They don't know enough about birds, and they haven't been back to Briddvale since Christmas. This is someone new."

"It's good that Ava and Tippi are coming tomorrow," Jack said. "When the seven of us put our heads together, no criminal is safe."

There was a knock and Jack's bedroom door opened. "Jack, I— Oh! Twitch!" Jack's dad was startled to see him. "I didn't know you were here."

"Hello, Mr Cappleman." Twitch stood up. "I came to talk to Jack about the Easter holidays, but I should be going."

"You can stay the night if you want," Jack said. "He can, can't he, Dad? It's the holidays."

"I have to go home," Twitch told him. "I've got my paper round in the morning, but I'll see you at the station, to meet Ava and Tippi's train."

"I'll drive you, Twitch," Mr Cappleman offered. "It's too dark for you to walk. I'll just go get my keys."

As the door closed, Twitch turned to his friend. "Jack, egg thieves target the rarest birds. They do terrible damage to vulnerable populations. We have to catch this thief quickly. It's spring. Nesting season. The birds in Briddvale are in danger!"

3
EARLY BIRDS

Jack's alarm screamed at him from under his pillow. He turned it off and threw the covers back without opening his eyes. It was dark, but it didn't matter because he was already dressed. Sitting up, he turned on his bedside lamp, blinking against the brightness as he shoved his feet into his trainers. His rucksack was packed beside his bedroom door. He pulled on his coat, slipped the bag over his shoulder and crept downstairs. He left a pre-written note on the kitchen table, went to the fridge and took out a freezer bag containing the chocolate spread sandwiches he'd made last night. Wheeling his bike from the garage, Jack set off.

By the time Jack reached Twitch's house, the sky was the greenish shade of dark blue that heralds the rising sun. Taking out his phone, he typed: *You up yet? I'm outside your front door.*

Two minutes later, Twitch opened the door in his pyjamas.

"Surprise!" Jack whispered, enjoying the baffled look on his friend's face.

"What are you doing here? It's five-thirty in the morning!"

"I've got something to show you. I would've shown you last night, only I forgot because of the egg thief. Can I come in? It's freezing out here."

"I've got about thirty minutes before I have to get ready to do my paper round," Twitch said in a hushed voice, ushering Jack down the hall and into the kitchen.

"I'm doing it with you. I've got my bike. We'll get it done quicker together and then we can work on the case." Jack noticed there were shadows under Twitch's eyes. "You all right?"

"I couldn't sleep," Twitch replied. "Then I had bad dreams."

"About the peregrine falcons?"

Twitch's lips pressed together in a narrow line as he nodded. "Sometimes I think human beings are horrible. I wish I wasn't one."

"Some of us are nice." Jack gave Twitch's arm a gentle shove.

"I know." Twitch sighed. "But, when I see a rare bird,

I have sad thoughts, like … this might be the only time I ever see this bird because they'll be gone one day." His expression was haunted. "Maybe soon."

"Don't think like that," Jack said softly. "Concentrate on the good things people are doing to make a difference, like us, like the Twitchers." He gave him a reassuring smile. "I've got something that will cheer you up." From his rucksack he carefully lifted a white plastic dish with a black microphone in its centre. Pulling headphones over his head, he plugged them into a chunky rectangular recorder strapped onto his belt and waggled it at Twitch. "It arrived yesterday when we were at school."

"Is that a parabolic microphone?" Twitch looked impressed. "Have you tried it?"

"I thought we could test it together."

Twitch glanced up at the kitchen clock. "Have you had breakfast?"

"Brought it with me." Jack whipped the bag of sandwiches out of his pocket.

"Give me a second to get dressed." Twitch hared away and Jack sat down at the table to eat his sandwiches. He thought about how down Twitch was and decided that, until they could meet the others, he would distract and cheer up his friend.

Twitch returned, dressed in combats and a hoodie,

and hurriedly poured milk onto a bowl of cereal. Unlocking his back door, he grabbed his bowl and waved Jack through. "I'll eat in the garden. You can try the microphone."

"According to the instructions, this parabolic microphone can capture sounds from fifty or sixty metres away. I just need some birds to record."

"You came to the right place." Twitch strolled past Jack, stopping beneath the old wild lilac tree from which dangled an assortment of brightly coloured chipped and broken teapots. Twitch had made the tree to cheer up his mum after his grandparents had died. The broken crockery had been turned into bird feeders, baths and nesting boxes. Jack watched as his friend closed his eyes and listened.

Lifting his left hand, Twitch pointed towards a neighbouring garden. "Blackbirds. Two of them."

Pulling his headphones on, Jack directed the white dish to where Twitch had indicated. With a thrill of excitement, he heard two birds trilling their penny whistle duet loud and clear. He pressed record on the box strapped to his belt. "Got them!"

Between mouthfuls of cereal, Twitch waved his spoon. "Wren. Over there."

Jack moved the dish, tuned in to the bird's song,

and hit record. Twitch's ability to instantly recognize a bird by its call seemed miraculous to Jack, like a superpower. "Come and listen," he said. "It's captured it brilliantly!"

The boys huddled together as they took turns putting the headphones on and playing back the blackbirds and the wren.

"That's so cool!" Twitch smiled and Jack was relieved to see the shadow of his earlier mood retreating.

A squawking came through the headphones. Beyond the chicken-wire fence at the bottom of the garden was an old outhouse that had been converted into a chicken coop. Twitch's three hens were inside clucking excitedly. Jack pointed the white dish in their direction. "Eggbum, Dodo and Fandango say they're hungry."

Twitch rolled his eyes. "Those hens are always hungry."

"I've been learning more about the Dracula parrot," Jack said, following Twitch into the chicken run.

"You're not still trying to build a Horror Lifer List?" Twitch chuckled. Jack's approach to birdwatching was different to Twitch's. Whereas Twitch was interested in all birds, Jack was drawn to birds of prey. Since he'd discovered his spark bird, a bearded vulture, he'd been making a new kind of list, containing birds that he thought were deadly cool. He kept a list of all the birds he'd spotted, like every other birder, but Jack's particular passion was for birds that could star in horror movies.

"The Dracula parrot is forty-five centimetres tall," Jack said, as Twitch filled the chicken's food trough, "with a normal parrot body but a head like a vulture's! Its plumage is black and scarlet, like Dracula's cloak."

"Does it suck blood?" Twitch chuckled and Jack's heart lifted at the sound.

"Sadly, no. It eats fruit. Figs mostly." Jack pretended to be sad about this.

"Are you sure you haven't confused it with a gracula?"

"What? Wait! There's a bird called Gracula! How did I not know that?" Jack took out his notebook and pen. "That's going on the Horror Lifer List for sure."

"What birds do you have so far?" Twitch asked, dusting off his hands.

"Dracula parrots, ravens, crows, vultures, falcons…" Jack kicked himself silently as Twitch's expression clouded over at the mention of the bird who'd fallen foul of the egg thief. "Er, eagles, *graculas*" – he made a show of adding the new bird to the list – "oh, and seagulls."

"No such thing," Twitch said flatly, as he came out of the chicken coop.

"There is," Jack insisted.

"Nope. There are different types of gull, like a herring gull or the black-headed gull. They all get called seagulls, but there's no such bird."

"Well, I say there is," Jack argued, "and they're terrifying. When I was little, we went on holiday to the seaside. Brighton. We went on the pier. My mum bought me a bag of hot mini doughnuts coated in sugar—"

"They're nice."

"I love them. Anyway, I was walking along, eating one, and a massive seagull swooped down and snatched it out of my hand! Then, the evil bird swooped around, came back and grabbed the whole bag! I thought it was going to carry me off next. I was so scared I cried! My mum had to take me back to the hotel."

"Bet it was a herring gull." Twitch laughed. "Hey, maybe that's why it took you a while to get into birdwatching? Too scared of them!"

"I'm not the only person to find birds scary. There's a horror movie called *The Birds*, you know. It's really old. We should watch it. Loads of birds attack a bunch of people trapped in an old house."

"All right." Twitch grinned. "So long as you don't mind if I'm on the side of the birds."

THE BIRDS AND THE TREES

Jack raced Twitch to Mr Bettany's newsagent's, which stood at the point where Briddvale Road became the high street, not far from their school. The morning was fresh and frosty, the sky was an icy blue and the pair were neck and neck all the way to the shop. Twitch pulled on his brakes, turned into the skid, and neatly slotted his BMX into the bike rack at the same time as jumping off.

"Unfair advantage!" Jack cried as Twitch did a victory dance. "You've had practice."

The bell tinkled as Twitch pushed the door open. Jack saw Mr Bettany kneeling on the floor, counting newspapers from a stack. He raised a forefinger to his flat cap in greeting, his lips monitoring his counting. He pointed a pencil at two hessian bags heavy with the Saturday papers. Twitch picked them up, passing one to Jack, and said, "I've got a helper today."

Mr Bettany scribbled something in the margin of a newspaper before smiling up at them. "Me too." He nodded to the counter. Behind it, standing in front of jars of boiled sweets, was Pippa. "You know my granddaughter Pippa, don't you, Twitch?"

Pippa's face turned pink as she waved.

"Yes." Twitch glanced at Jack. "Hi, Pippa."

"Are you going to Aves Wood today?" Pippa asked.

"Er…" Twitch spoke hurriedly. "Not sure yet. Are we, Jack? We're meeting our friends at the station in a bit. We'd better go. Lots of papers to deliver. Bye."

"Bye!" Jack echoed, suppressing a giggle as they piled out the door and jumped back on their bikes before Pippa could ask another question.

"Where do you think we should begin our investigation?" Twitch asked Jack, as they pedalled back towards the crossroads, slower now that they were loaded down with heavy bags. Jack noticed the intense expression on Twitch's face, and it occurred to him that if he didn't catch the egg thief, his best friend might not ever forgive him.

"Once we've met Ava and Tippi's train, I think we should go straight up to Passerine Pike," Jack replied, pushing his fears aside. "The police will have finished their search of the crime scene. Now it's our turn."

Conversation became tougher as the gradient of the north road grew steep.

"The fastest way … to get the paper round done," Twitch said, between gasps, "is to go to the furthest house … and work back … then it's downhill all the way."

Within the hour, the boys were racing back to the newsagent's to exchange their empty bags for a small brown envelope containing Twitch's wages.

"It's a bit after seven-thirty," Twitch said, as they climbed back onto their bikes. "We've two hours before Ava and Tippi arrive. Should we do some investigating now?"

"I think we should wait for the others before we go to the pike," Jack said. "But how about we go to Aves Wood and scout about. We may see someone hunting for nests, or acting suspicious. The egg thief is hardly going to return to the scene of the crime. Most likely they'll be where birds are nesting. We can test my microphone at the same time."

Twitch didn't look impressed with this plan. He was obviously keen to get back to the falcons' nest and hunt for clues, but he reluctantly agreed.

As they crossed Crowther Bridge, Jack spotted something that sent his heartbeat into a canter. He yanked on his brakes, stopping suddenly. "Look!" he whispered, nodding down at a grey-haired man in wading trousers, navy shirt and a beige, pocketed waistcoat who was setting up for a day of fishing. Several rods were laid out on the grass beside him. He was arranging his tackle box and two camping chairs.

"He's got the waistcoat and the fishing rods! Is he the man you saw on Passerine Pike, the night the eggs went missing?"

Twitch shook his head. "I've never seen him before."

"Oh." Jack's shoulders dropped with disappointment.

"The man on the pike was younger and skinnier," Twitch said, keeping his voice low, as they watched the fisherman pick up a rod in his gloved hands. "I wonder who he is. I know most of the people who fish the canal and the river."

"He could be a suspect," Jack whispered, clinging to the excitement he'd felt when he'd first spotted the waistcoat.

The man settled down in one of his chairs and peered into his tackle box.

"Maybe," Twitch said, sounding doubtful.

"Let's go talk to him." Jack got off his bike, wheeling it towards the towpath. "Morning," he called cheerily as he approached the stranger. "Lovely day for a spot of fishing."

"Let's hope so." The man looked up at the sky as if he feared it was going to cloud over.

Jack wondered what question he could ask that would reveal whether this man was an egger. "Er … are you on holiday?"

"I suppose I am." The man looked amused by this idea.

"It's just, we come to the woods all the time," Jack said. "We know all the people who fish here." Realizing his statement sounded like an accusation, he gave the man a friendly smile. "My name's Jack, and this is Twitch."

"Twitch! That's an unusual name."

"His *real* name is Corvus," Jack explained, delighted to have found a way to turn the conversation to birds, "but everyone calls him Twitch on account of him being a mega birdwatcher."

The fisherman stretched out a gloved hand and shook each of theirs. "You like birds do you, Twitch? A fine hobby. I'm Merle Drake, more of a fisher than a birder, I'm afraid. And you're right. I'm not from these parts. I live in Cornwall."

"Merle! Merle," came a woman's voice. "There's a cafe in the nature reserve visitor centre. It's not open yet, but the woman inside made me two teas and said I could pay her later." A rosy-cheeked woman in walking boots, wearing a brown wax jacket and burgundy fedora hat, waddled onto the towpath carrying two steaming cups. "Oh!" She smiled warmly at Twitch and Jack. "Hello."

"Evelyn dear, this is Jack and Twitch. They're local boys." He turned to them. "And this is Mrs Drake. Now, you must tell me something." He narrowed his eyes. "Either of your dads fish?" He grunted in satisfaction when they both shook their heads. "You're not here to check out the competition then?"

"What competition?" Jack asked.

"Don't listen to him," Evelyn Drake said, bustling through to sit in the vacant camping chair. "Merle's here for the big Canal Masters fishing competition," she explained. "I'm surprised you don't know about it!"

"We're birdwatchers," Twitch told her.

"Oh, how lovely! I'm a big fan of our feathered friends." She beamed. "I'm no birder, mind, but I do love to watch them in my garden."

"Twitch knows more about birds than anyone in Briddvale," Jack said proudly. "We've got a club, called the Twitchers. We watch birds and solve crimes."

"Well, isn't that something!" She chuckled and took

40

a sip of her tea. "Just like the Famous Five, I'll bet."

"Except we're real," Jack told her, annoyed that she wasn't taking him seriously. "We solved the case of Robber Ryan last summer…"

"…and uncovered an illegal plot to hunt raptors," Twitch added.

"We were in all the papers," Jack said.

"Gosh." Mrs Drake looked impressed. "Well, I know who to come to if I have a mystery that needs solving!"

"We're working on a case right now, actually," Jack boasted. "We'd better get going."

They said goodbye to the Drakes and pushed their bikes onto the footpath into Aves Wood.

"Twitch," Jack said, as an idea struck him. "What if the egg thief is someone from out of town, come for this fishing competition?"

"That would make sense!" Twitch's features lit up. "I was thinking, last night, that if someone local was stealing eggs from birds' nests, for their secret collection, I'd know about it. I mean, I spend so much of my time watching the local birds, I think I'd notice if eggs were disappearing, and big thefts would be reported in the papers."

"Are these the first eggs you've known to be stolen?"

"Yes."

"Mmm … interesting." Jack took out the notebook he was using for the case and scribbled something down as Twitch locked their bikes to a fence post in the car park. "I think we need to find out who's entering this fishing competition."

With his mind churning, Jack led the way through the west gate and into the nature reserve. There was something special about Aves Wood. Jack felt it every time he was amongst the trees. The noise and bustle of everyday life melted away. A distant electricity pylon, standing like a mini Eiffel Tower on a bit of scrubland beyond the River Bridd, was the only reminder that an outside world even existed. Inside the woods, he could hear the river gurgling like a happy baby. Above him, beyond the latticework of scantily clad branches, was a powder-blue sky with clouds as white and puffy as a child's drawing. Emerging bluebells lent a cobalt tinge to the intensely green forest floor. A solitary bee with copper hairs on its back – a mining bee, Twitch told him – flew past, hunting for willow catkins and dandelions. Jack's spirits rose. He felt alive.

It's spring! It's spring! Brrrr-uppp! Brrrr-uppp! Brrrr-uppp! the birds sang.

Twitch stopped abruptly, signalling that Jack should get out his microphone.

"Chiffchaff?" Jack asked, as he pointed the microphone dish at the loud tweeter.

Twitch smiled and nodded.

Jack inhaled the scent of damp earth, tree sap and dewy moss. "It really feels like spring is here!"

"For me, spring starts when the swallows have returned," Twitch said, his eyes turning upwards. "Which should be any day now."

Jack thought back to last summer and the piping squeaks of the swallow chicks that had emanated from the nest their parents had built beside Twitch's open bedroom window. It had seemed peculiar and marvellous to him that they came back every year. But after what had happened to the peregrine falcon nest, Jack thought the swallows were clever. There was no safer place in the whole of Briddvale to raise a clutch of chicks than Twitch's bedroom.

"The swallows will be on their migration flight from Africa," Twitch said. "It's such a long way. I'm always nervous until they arrive safely."

He stiffened, pricking up his ears, a look of alert amazement on his face.

"What is it?" Jack whispered. Twitch grabbed his right hand and steered the microphone, pointing it up at the canopy. Through his headphones Jack heard a strange call, like the whistle of a World War II bomb being dropped from a plane. Then came the racket of high-pitched machine-gun fire. He could see from the expression on Twitch's face, this was a special bird. He pressed record.

"Nightingale!" Twitch exhaled the word like a sigh and reached into his trouser pockets. Confused, he patted his other pockets, then checked his rucksack. Horror dawned on his face. "Oh, no! Jack! My binoculars!" He was pale. "I had them last night. I must've dropped them when I ran to yours."

"Then we'll find them." Jack knew the binoculars were precious. They had once belonged to Twitch's grandad, who'd inspired his love of birds. "Once we've met Ava and Tippi's train, all seven of us will search the whole of Passerine Pike. They won't be lost for very long."

Twitch nodded, but his haunted expression had returned.

"What do nightingales look like?" Jack asked, hoping to distract him.

"Small, brown…"

"Why so many birds gotta be small and brown!" Jack exclaimed. "How am I supposed to identify them?"

Twitch gave a half-hearted snort.

"How come nightingales are thought to be special if they look like other songbirds and sound like they're playing war games?"

"The song of the nightingale can be strange but it's changeable. The birds mimic sounds and adapt their song. It's the unpredictable and sometimes bonkers nature of the nightingale's music that makes it wonderful." Twitch paused to listen to the bird in the canopy. "This one is calling to attract a mate. If it doesn't find one here, it'll move on."

"How cool would it be to have a nesting pair of nightingales in Aves Wood?" Jack said. "Imagine the singing from a clutch of baby nightingales!"

"There'll only be baby nightingales if no one steals their eggs," Twitch said grimly. "We've got to catch that thief, Jack."

5

WHAM! BAM!

Twitch's footsteps echoed off the tiled floor as he walked through Briddvale Station. The quaint red-brick building was adorned with old-fashioned signs and had a triangular lead roof from which hung baskets stuffed with miniature daffodils, hyacinths and trailing ivy. On the platform, above the benches for waiting passengers, hung replica gas lamps fitted with electric bulbs. An iron footbridge took you over the rails. Twitch visited it often to watch the birds in the woodland flanking the tracks.

"You're here!" Jack cried out to the three people sitting on the platform bench.

Their heads turned. The long black hair belonged to Tara Dabiri. She flashed them a wide smile, her brown eyes sparkling with anticipation. Twitch knew she couldn't wait for Ava and Tippi to arrive. Ozuru Sawa

46

waved in greeting, his neatly cropped, bowl-shaped, locks framing his calm and friendly face. Twitch saw the sleepy scrunched-up expression behind Terry Vallis's dark springy curls and guessed he wasn't quite awake yet. Terry didn't like early mornings.

Jack bounced over to them, immediately launching into the story of Twitch's adventures at Passerine Pike.

"An egg thief!" Terry said, sounding bemused, as Tara's hands flew to her face in horror.

"Is it true?" Ozuru asked Twitch, and Twitch nodded gravely.

"We're on a mission," Jack said. "We've got to catch that thief and stop them from stealing any more eggs."

"Ava and Tippi will be able to help," Tara said.

"Ava's brilliant with stuff like this," Terry agreed. "She's fearless. Tippi's only nine though. Not sure how much help she'll be."

"Nine, and tougher than you, Terry," Jack said, laughing.

"Don't underestimate Tippi," Ozuru said.

"She's the most creative, wilful and stubborn kid I've ever met." Tara nodded.

"As soon as they arrive," Jack said, "we're going to Passerine Pike to investigate the scene of the crime."

"Jack, can I borrow your binoculars?" Twitch asked.

"I want to go up on the bridge; see if anything interesting is nesting."

"Where are yours?" Terry sounded surprised.

"I lost them last night."

"Not your grandad's bins!" Terry was wide awake now. They all knew how much those binoculars meant to Twitch.

"We're going to find them today," Jack said, handing his over.

Jogging up the iron steps, Twitch lifted the binoculars and swept the horizon for the distinctive forked tail of the swallow. The town of Briddvale was nestled in a valley. The rolling emerald patchwork of lush fields, spotted with dark areas of forest, rose before him. The swallows could arrive any day now, unless the weather had been bad, or they'd been attacked by larger birds, or got tangled up with air traffic! It was a six-thousand-mile journey from the bottom of Africa to Briddvale, fraught with risk and peril. It always felt like a miracle when they arrived. Twitch could do with a miracle right now.

Somewhere out there, he thought, is an egg thief looking for another opportunity to add to their collection. Twitch's anger was cooler today. He felt it strengthening his bones. He was going to do everything in his power to bring down that cold-hearted egger, whoever they were.

"What time will the train arrive?" he heard Terry asking Tara for the third time.

"Nine thirty-seven," Tara answered, looking at her phone. "In eleven minutes."

Twitch smiled to himself. Tara was so patient. It was one of her many endearing qualities.

"What are you guys doing on Easter Sunday?" Jack asked.

"We don't do Easter," Tara replied. "I'm Muslim."

"Lucky," Terry grumbled. "I had to give up stuff for Lent *and* I have to go to Mass on Easter Sunday."

"But that's in the morning, right?" Jack asked.

"Yeah. Early." Terry's expression showed that he thought Sunday mornings were for sleeping.

"What did you give up for Lent?" Tara asked him.

"Liver," Terry said.

"You hate liver!" Ozuru said.

Terry grinned. "Exactly."

"We don't go to church at Easter," Jack said. He paused, suddenly looking sheepish. "My mum's been complaining that I'm always in the woods, or at Twitch's house, and I never invite you guys over."

"Yeah," Terry joked. "What's that about?"

"She wants to host an Easter egg hunt in our garden, next Sunday," Jack went on, ignoring him. "I told her it was babyish but…"

"Will the eggs be chocolate?" Terry looked immediately interested.

"What else would they be?" Jack asked.

"In our house, we get one teeny weeny chocolate egg each," Terry said. "If I don't eat all of it immediately, I lose it. My brothers steal it. I hid my egg last year. Gareth found it and ate the whole thing in front of me." He grimaced. "It's rubbish being the youngest of seven."

"You can have one of mine," Ozuru offered. "I get loads."

"I think an egg hunt would be fun," Tara said. "Tippi would love it. We won't be doing anything Easter-ish in my house. Ava's bringing their eggs, but on actual Easter Day Tippi's bound to miss her mum. An egg hunt would be great."

Twitch was listening to their chatter when a movement in the trees near the bench caught his eye. Thinking it might be a bird, he retrained the binoculars and saw a flash of red. Zeroing in, he was surprised to find he was looking at Clem Buckskin, a short athletic boy from their class at school. He was wearing a checked shirt, jeans, and lying along a bough of the tree clutching a small red balloon in one hand and a phone in the other. Scanning down the tree trunk, Twitch glimpsed blonde hair. A girl, Pamela Hardacre, was hiding behind it and peeping out.

"The train!" Jack called out, jumping up from the bench. "I see it."

"They're here!" Tara said, clapping her hands together as she rose to join him.

Pamela waved an instruction to Clem just as the train stopped at the platform, blocking Twitch's view of his friends. Twitch dashed back over the bridge. "Jack! Watch out!" he called, pointing to Clem in the tree, but no one heard him over the beeping of the opening doors. He ran down the steps.

Standing in the open doorway, Twitch saw Ava, dressed in black joggers, trainers and a puffy coat, holding the hand of her little sister Tippi, who was wearing a rainbow of colours. They bounded off the train, rucksacks bobbing on their backs. Tippi threw her arms around Tara, hugging her. Ava smiled shyly at Jack. Behind the girls, a stocky man stepped down from the train, finding his way blocked by the excited children. Ozuru noticed and stepped aside, grabbing Terry and turning him around just as Clem hurled the red balloon.

"Look out!" Twitch shouted.

Terry looked up in time to see the wobbling red missile right before it hit him on the forehead with a loud *slap!* It burst, drenching him, and spraying the others with water, including the unfortunate stocky man.

"Aargh!" Terry yelped in shock and the others cried out in dismay.

Pamela Hardacre sprang out from behind the tree holding a microphone. Clem was pointing the phone camera at her. With her back to the Twitchers, Pam crowed, "Wham! Bam! They just got pranked by Pam!"

"You!" Terry howled, dashing towards her.

Pam squealed, sprinting away down the platform, laughing. "Keep filming!" she called to Clem.

Beyond Pam, Twitch spotted an elfin face peeking around the station entrance. His heart sank. It was Pippa Bettany. She was following him again. Pippa shrank back and disappeared as Pam ran towards her.

Gasping for breath, Terry gave up chasing Pam. Instead, he turned to the tree in which Clem was sitting. "You absolute, utter and complete—" He angrily kicked the trunk. "Ouch!" he yelped, grabbing his foot. "That hurt."

Clem grinned. He was still filming.

"You come down here right now" – Terry shook a fist at him – "and I'll, I'll…"

"You'll what?" Clem asked, sounding mildly interested. Terry wasn't a fighter. They all knew that. Clem, on the other hand, was captain of the school football team and didn't mind getting physical when trying to win the ball. "Cheer up, Terry. It was only a joke. You can take a joke, can't you?"

"Easy for you to say," Terry snapped back, looking down at his sodden clothes. He shook himself, like a dog. Several curls were stuck to his forehead and there was a red mark where the balloon had burst against his pale skin. "You're not the one that got completely soaked."

Twitch saw that there was a spray of mist sitting on the thick black curls of the stocky man who'd had the misfortune to get off the train behind Ava and Tippi. He had on a giant backpack and was wheeling a tackle box the size of a small suitcase.

"I am so sorry, sir," Ozuru said, moving out of his way. Everyone stepped back, aware that they might be in big trouble.

"It's just water," the man said, giving the children a warm smile. "My friends have done plenty worse to me."

"That girl is *not* our friend," Terry informed him. "She's a living nightmare!"

The man laughed.

"Are you here for the Canal Masters?" Ozuru asked, pointing to the tackle box. "My dad's entering. He's really excited. It's his first time."

"I do it every year. The Masters is an excuse for me to spend a week fishing and discovering a new part of the countryside." He extended his hand. "I'm Chris Merriman."

"I'm Ozuru Sawa." He gestured to the others. "These are my friends, Terry, Tara, Ava, Tippi, Twitch and Jack."

"Welcome to Briddvale," Jack said with a wry smile.

"I don't suppose you know how I can get to Patchem's farm campsite?" Chris Merriman asked. "I thought there'd be taxis at the station…"

They all glanced towards the empty road beyond the building.

"It's about a half-hour walk," Twitch told him.

"I can give you the number of a minicab company," Tara offered, getting out her phone.

She read the number to a grateful Chris Merriman and by the time they'd turned back to Clem's tree, it was empty.

"He had a lucky escape," Terry said, weakly waving a bunched-up fist.

"Forget Clem," Ava declared, throwing up her hands. "We're here! At last!"

6

CANAL MASTERS

Twitch fell into step beside Terry as they walked out of the station. "I'm sorry, Terry. I tried to warn everyone."

"It's my fault," Tara said, taking out a tissue and mopping Terry's dripping chin. "I meant to tell everyone that Pam's on the prowl, but I was so excited about Ava and Tippi coming, I forgot."

"On the prowl?" Terry's eyebrows rose.

"The other day, at school, Sybil told me that Pam's YouTube channel is losing followers because she hasn't found any crimes to report. She thinks funny videos will get viewers back. She's persuaded Clem to help her film pranks."

"Yeah, well, she's going to regret picking on us," Terry said. He turned and loudly pronounced to the group, "No one is allowed to tell Pam about the egg thief. Got that? She targets us with water bombs" – he swiped the air dramatically – "she doesn't get the scoop on the Twitchers' new case."

"What new case?" Ava asked, looking at Jack. "What egg thief?" She turned to Twitch. "What's going on?"

"Five eggs have been stolen from a peregrine falcon nest on Passerine Pike," Twitch told her. "The police were up there yesterday."

"Poor mummy and daddy falcons!" Tippi exclaimed, her forehead creasing with distress.

"There is an egg thief in Briddvale," Jack said gravely. "But we will find them and stop them."

"We're planning to go straight up to Passerine Pike now, to investigate," Twitch said. "If that's all right with you?"

"There's nothing I'd rather do," Ava said, and Tippi nodded.

"But I'm soaking wet!" Terry wailed, holding out the hem of his sweater and pointing at his jeans. "It'll be freezing up there."

"I can help with that." Ava slid her rucksack off her back and unzipped it. "We're about the same height. You can choose between black leggings, or purple trackie-bottoms. And you can borrow this." She held up a lavender-grey hoodie.

"Why can't I wear your black tracksuit?" Terry said, pointing at the clothes Ava was wearing.

"Because I am!" Ava raised an eyebrow. "Do you want dry clothes or not?"

"I am not wearing your leggings."

"Fine. Here." Ava shoved the purple trousers and hoodie at him. "Go and get changed, and hurry up. We've got an egg thief to catch."

"Nobody's allowed to look!" Terry called out, running into the trees by the road.

"Like we'd want to," Ava said, rolling her eyes.

"Thank goodness Pam's gone." Tara giggled. "Bet she'd love to video Terry right now."

Jack laughed. Ozuru, who was Terry's best friend, tried to give him a stern look whilst simultaneously stifling his own laughter and snorted, which set Twitch off.

A moment later, Terry emerged from the trees, a vision in purple. "These trousers are really warm and soft!" he said, looking delighted with his outfit.

"You look lovely," Ava said.

Twitch pulled a folded bag from his pocket for Terry to put his wet clothes in.

"Right, let's go," Jack cried.

Half an hour later, the seven Twitchers were standing in a huddle in Passerine Pike car park.

"Jack," Twitch said, "I just remembered. There was a silver car here last night. A VW Golf. A man was sitting in it. He had a shaved head. He seemed to be watching the police."

"That's suspicious," Ava said.

"Was the car here the night before?" Jack took out his notebook. "The night the eggs were stolen?"

"I don't think so." Twitch thought back. "I don't remember seeing any cars. And I didn't recognize the man."

"Don't suppose you caught the number plate?" Jack said, writing something in his notebook.

"No. I ran past it really fast."

"Shall I make an investigation timeline?" Ozuru suggested. "I could start on Thursday the twenty-eighth of March, when the eggs were stolen, and mark important things, like when the police investigated, or when Twitch was here, and today, if we find clues."

"Oooh yes, you can add things people tell us in interviews, like their alibis," Ava said.

"If there are more egg thefts," Terry said, "we can mark them on it too."

"I've got a horrible feeling there will be," Twitch said, his stomach dropping at the thought. "Egg collectors are obsessive, and spring is when most birds are nesting and laying."

"Temptation will be everywhere," Tara agreed.

"The timeline is a great idea," Jack said. "Ozuru, what can you tell us about this fishing competition you were talking to Chris Merriman about?"

"The Canal Masters is an annual nationwide fishing competition. For the first time ever, one of the early heats is taking place along the Briddvale Canal. It starts on Monday."

"This morning," Twitch said, "we met a married couple who've come from Cornwall to take part in it. And on Thursday evening, I saw a tall, skinny, chalky-haired man up here with a fishing rod strapped to his rucksack."

"Twitch thinks our egg thief may be from out of town," Jack told them all.

"If an egg thief lived in Briddvale," Twitch said, "I'm certain I'd already know about it."

"Lots of people will be coming to Briddvale because of the Canal Masters," Ozuru said.

"Right then, we'll need to find out who's taking part," Jack said, "and learn everything we can about them."

"The first fishing day is Monday," Ozuru said, "but most serious competitors will be fishing the canal this weekend, to get a feel for it."

"How does the competition work?" Ava asked.

"You pay to enter," Ozuru said, "then you're given a peg, in a draw..."

"What's a peg?" Tippi asked.

"A pitch, a place along the canal that you fish from. The pegs are numbered and spaced about five metres apart, so no one is fishing anyone else's patch. The competitors fish for five hours – or something like that – and at the end of the day your fish are weighed. Everyone is ranked according to how much fish they've caught."

"And the winner goes through to the next round?" Ava guessed.

"No." Ozuru lifted a finger. "Fishing is a lot to do with luck, so there's a second day. A few days later, everyone goes through the same process. You are allowed to enter the weight of your biggest catch on either day. Whoever catches the most fish is the winner of the heat. The top two people go through to the next round, which takes place on a different canal. The tournament goes on through spring and then summer. The Canal Master is announced right at the end."

"I've never been fishing," Tara said. "Is it fun?"

"It's like bird-spotting," Ozuru replied. "Anyone can spot a bird, but it takes time to recognize and learn about habitats, diet and all that stuff. It's the same with fish."

"It looks like a lot of sitting around to me," Jack admitted.

"Fishing is classified as a sport, I think," Ozuru said. "But it's more like an art. A good fisherman is impressive to watch."

"Are there fisherwomen?" Tara asked.

"Oh yes." Ozuru nodded. "The local person to beat in this heat of the Canal Masters is Beryl Crocker. She came third in the whole competition last year. She's the best fisherman, I mean fisherwoman, er, fisherperson in Briddvale. Everyone knows that."

"Old Mrs Crocker who takes the collection in church every Sunday?" Terry asked, and Ozuru nodded.

"Dad says that Beryl Crocker's husband used to fish but wouldn't let her do it. I don't think it was thought of as ladylike in those days."

"Ladylike," Ava scoffed. "What rot!"

"He died and had his ashes scattered in the River Bridd. The next day, Beryl Crocker took his fishing tackle, went to the river and cast a line. People joke that she took up fishing to get her husband back."

"Because the fishes ate him?" Tippi's eyes were wide.

"And she became a champion fisher?" Tara looked delighted by this turn of events.

"She's won loads of prizes." Ozuru nodded. "There

are always stories about her in the *Briddvale Record*. She is way better than her husband was."

"I've read about her," Jack said.

"Have you?" Twitch was surprised.

"I read the paper every week," he replied. "To learn about the weird town I'm living in." He smiled. "And it's a good place to find crimes that need solving."

"You've lived in Briddvale for a year now," Twitch realized. It was odd to think back to a time when he hadn't known Jack. They were inseparable now.

"Yeah." Jack reached forward and lifted his binoculars from around Twitch's neck. "And look what you've done to me! You've turned me into a bird nerd!"

"I've made you cool." Twitch grinned.

"The last day of this round of the Canal Masters is Wednesday the third of April," Ozuru said. "If our suspect is from out of town, and they're only in Briddvale for the fishing competition, they'll probably be leaving on Thursday the fourth."

"That only gives us five days to catch our thief!" Jack said, looking alarmed.

Ava let out a low whistle. "We'd better get up that hill and start investigating."

7

EAGLE EYES

Jack held up his hands to get everyone's attention. "Let's split into groups," he said. "Ava, Tippi and I will go to the peak of the pike to hunt for clues. Ozuru, Terry, you circle the hill, paying careful attention to the paths the thief might've used. Tara, Twitch, you take the fence along the Mord Estate." Jack paused, noticing that Twitch wasn't paying attention but studying the ground. "We need to keep our eyes peeled, not just for clues, but also for Twitch's binoculars." Twitch shot him a grateful smile. "If you spot something interesting, give a shout. OK. Let's go."

"Have you any idea who we're looking for?" Ava asked him as they climbed the hill.

"No, and we have to remember that the police have tramped all over the place, but Twitch and I have built a profile of the unknown perp…"

"Unknown perp?" Ava shot Jack a wry sideways look. "You've been watching too many American cop shows."

Jack chose to ignore this dig. "Let's pretend," he said, as they approached the abandoned nest, "that I'm the thief. I scoped out the nest earlier in the day and worked out how I was going to get to it. Now, it's dark. It's night. I've come back to steal the falcon eggs." He closed his fist, miming holding a torch. "I'd have a torch, but I'd keep it pointed at the ground. I don't want people to see the light."

"You might have one of those hooded torches, that have side shutters to direct the beam," Ava suggested.

"Yes, especially if stealing eggs is something I do a lot." Jack shivered. The top of the hill was exposed, and an icy wind was blowing.

"Terry and Ozuru won't find anything round there." Tippi pointed at the boys, who were on the grassy side of the hill. "The egg thief will have used the path we just came up."

"How do you know?" Jack asked.

"Because the ground is like a big wet sponge." She bounced on the sodden turf for emphasis. "On the grass, they would leave footprints. The path is hard, all flinty and chalky. No footprints. And it's the fastest way up here."

"Excellent detecting, Tippi!" Jack was impressed by her deduction. He smiled as Tippi danced a couple of steps in response to his praise.

"The moon is only just on the wane," Ava said, looking up from her phone. "Two nights ago, there will have been moonlight to see by."

"Here is where I would turn my torch off." Jack pointed to the curve in the path. "So I don't alarm the birds."

"You're thinking like Twitch, not an egg thief," Ava told him. "The thief wouldn't care about alarming the birds. They may have even used the torch to frighten them away from the nest."

"Of course," Jack chided himself. "I'd shine the torch right at the birds." He pointed his fist up at the ledge where the empty nest sat. "But I wouldn't want to use a loud noise to scare them away, in case it brought people running."

"You've got to get the falcons away from the nest if you want to steal their eggs," Ava said.

"Do you think that would be hard?"

"I'm not sure," Ava admitted. "Twitch might know."

They turned and looked across at Twitch and Tara, who were searching around the base of the hawthorn tree. "We'll ask him in a bit. I'm going to climb up to the nest," Jack said. "Take a look inside."

At first, as he clambered up the big rocks, Jack made good progress. He was aware of Ava and Tippi watching him. However, the closer he got to the nest, the fewer handholds and footholds he could find. He came to a spot where he was stuck and remembered Twitch saying the police had used climbing gear. The muscles in his legs began to shake and he felt a tremor of panic. He was really high up.

"You're nearly there," Ava called out. "Push yourself a bit higher. There's a little ledge you can put your left foot on. A bit higher. That's it. Now fling your foot out. Further. That's it. You've got it!"

Jack followed Ava's instructions and spotted a shelf of stone next to the nest. He reached it and half sat, half clung to the rock, trying not to look down. He knew that he could never have climbed up in the dark. He looked across at the hawthorn tree he'd viewed the nest from and saw Twitch up in its branches.

"My turn," Ava called out, running and jumping her way up the neighbouring rock with ease.

Jack was impressed, but felt mortified as he watched her ascend the adjacent rock. He realized Ava must have chosen her path before she'd started to climb. She seemed so confident of where to put her hands and feet.

"What can you see?" Tippi called up.

Jack turned his attention to the nest. A wave of nausea turned his stomach. A large flint was sitting on the woven twigs. Crushed beneath it was an eggshell. Spilling from it was a dead chick: a tiny, pink, prawn-like blob, covered in a congealed jelly. He felt a shock of sadness. Only two days ago, he and Twitch had been saying how they couldn't wait to see that chick hatch and fledge.

"Oh no," Ava whispered, seeing what he saw from the other side of the nest.

Remembering he was a detective, Jack pulled out his phone and took pictures of the crime scene. This chick had died in the nest, but the four others, its brothers or sisters, would also be dead, killed when the egg thief blew the eggs to empty the shells.

"Don't let Tippi see those pictures," Ava said in a hushed voice. "It'd break her heart."

"The thief threw a stone at the birds, to scare them away." Jack was so angry at this discovery, his resolve stiffened and his legs stopped trembling. When he found the egg thief, he was going to enjoy handing them over to the police.

"Look," Ava pointed at the rock in the nest. "It's covered in white dust. Do you think the police were looking for fingerprints?"

"Must've been," Jack replied, seeing the fine powder that had settled on the flint. "I guess they didn't find any or they would've taken the stone as evidence."

"So, our thief wears gloves," Ava remarked. "That's a clue of sorts."

"Don't you mean our *murderer* wears gloves." Jack was unable to take his eyes off the dead chick. "Twitch told me eggers were murderers, and I didn't really understand, but now I do."

The pair clambered down in silence.

"What did you see?" Tippi asked, bouncing on the balls of her feet, half in excitement, half to keep warm.

"Not much," Ava replied, putting a hand on her shoulder and steering her away from the rocks.

"Guys!" Terry called out, waving. "We've found something." He and Ozuru were standing beside a flat rock next to the path, halfway up the hill.

"What?" Jack asked, hurrying towards them.

"My binoculars?" Twitch asked hopefully. Ozuru shook his head and Twitch's face fell.

"I was thinking," Terry said, delighted to have everyone's attention, "if you had to get into a climbing harness or get out special tools for egg blowing, you might stop here." He sat down on the flat rock. "And, perhaps, you might have a little snack, to give you some strength."

"If you had to put gear on at night, surely you'd do it in your car?" Ava was shaking her head.

"A night-time egg heist is hardly a picnic," Tara agreed. "I'm not sure you'd bring snacks!"

"You don't know what the thief did," Ozuru huffed. "They might have had a snack."

"We found monkey-nut shells." Terry pointed down between his feet. "They look kind of fresh. They're not mouldy."

Jack knelt down. Sure enough there was a heap of empty peanut casings on the ground beside the rock.

"They could be from anyone," Twitch pointed out. "The police could've left them here."

"True," Jack said, whipping a freezer bag from his trouser pocket and pulling a pair of tweezers from inside his coat, "but they could also be a clue to our egg thief."

"Was there rain on Thursday evening?" Ava asked.

"It had stopped by seven-thirty," Tara replied. "That's when I was on my way back from dance class."

"It didn't rain yesterday," Twitch said.

"Not many people climb the pike in the rain," Terry said. "It's steep and gets very slippery."

"Which is why they would have used the path," Tippi said.

"These are mostly dry." Jack studied the peanut shells in the bag. "Any dampness is probably from the ground or morning dew."

"I was up here on Thursday when it started to rain," Twitch said. "It was torrential and then over. If they'd been on the ground then, they'd be mulch."

"It could've been someone else who ate the nuts, yesterday, after the eggs had already been taken," Tara said.

"I doubt many people have been up the pike this morning," Ozuru said. They all turned and looked about them. They couldn't see another soul. "If it's not the thief who dropped the peanut shells, then it's someone who came up the hill yesterday."

"Well, everyone needs to keep their eyes peeled for anyone who likes to eat monkey nuts," Jack said, putting the bag into his rucksack. "Or throws rocks at birds. We found one in the nest."

"Twitch, what would a peregrine falcon do if someone was trying to frighten it away from its nest?" Ava asked.

Twitch thought for a moment. "Both birds would protect the nest. They would dive-bomb, using their talons to attack, and if they got you, it would hurt. A lot."

Jack felt a bit of satisfaction at hearing this. He hoped the thief had got a good scratching. He looked up the hill, to the ledge and the nest. It would be hard to climb up there, in the dark, and take the eggs from the nest whilst being attacked by large, angry birds. The risk of falling or being injured would've been high.

"Our thief is dangerous," he said with a chilling certainty. "They'll risk everything to get what they want."

8

NEST WATCH

Jack saw Ava striding ahead of the group as they ambled onto the canal towpath and guessed she was eager to see the hide. He jogged to catch up with her.

"It feels good to be back in Briddvale," she said to him. "I don't even mind Pam being awful. That's how things should be." She chuckled. "Poor Terry. He did get that water balloon right splat in the face. There's still a red mark on his forehead where it burst."

"I don't think you're going to get your clothes back," Jack said, looking over his shoulder at the others. "Terry keeps going on about how comfy they are."

"I heard that!" Terry called out.

"Oh, I've missed this," Ava said, laughing. She threw out her hands, taking in the canal and the green hills beyond. "All of us, together. Here." Her hands fell to her sides. "Tippi and I sometimes worry you'll forget about us because we don't live in Briddvale and can only visit in the holidays."

"Forget you?" Jack was surprised to hear her say this. "Impossible! You're the reason the Twitchers exists!" He gestured to her and Tippi, who was talking nineteen-to-the-dozen at Tara. "You brought us together, on our first case. Have you any idea how excited we were when Tara announced you were coming for Easter? Ozuru actually squealed!"

Ozuru's shoulders lifted with embarrassment and his head shrank into his neck like a turtle's. "I was pleased," he admitted.

"I'm glad." Ava smiled at him.

"Wait till you see what we've done to the hide," Tara told her, as they took the path into Aves Wood.

Jack noticed that Twitch had fallen behind. He had been very quiet since they'd failed to find his binoculars. Jack tried to think of something cheering to say to his friend, but the image of the dead chick was at the forefront of his mind. He dropped back, falling into step beside Twitch as they entered Aves Wood via the kissing gate on the towpath. For a bit, they walked side by side in companionable silence.

"It doesn't look like we'll find my bins today," Twitch said, eventually.

"No." Jack gave him a sad smile. "But we won't stop looking."

Tippi pointed to the shopping trolley tree and made a show of looking around to make sure no one was coming. The old tree, which held the rusty old trolley in its branches, was the secret signpost to their hide. Certain the coast was clear, Tara held back the ferns and the line of Twitchers left the footpath, ducking low as they disappeared into the forest.

As they approached, Jack noticed that their club house, a construction of three rooms – a square shed, a tepee entrance, and a triangular two-man-tent-sized area – wasn't as hidden as it once had been. The floods last autumn had washed much of their camouflage away. He frowned. The hide was supposed to be the Twitchers' secret headquarters. People shouldn't be able to find it easily. He made a mental note: once they'd caught the egg thief, they would work on the camouflage.

"Oh!" Tippi bounded forward. "You've built a crow's nest! I see it! It looks amazing! I'm going up it right now." She ran to a tree beside the hide, unhooked a wooden coat hanger and yanked on it, opening a woven door of sticks and ferns in the tepee-shaped entrance hall. Once inside, Tippi went to the bottom of a ladder strapped to the trunk of the beech tree the hide was constructed around. The ladder stretched up through a hole in the roof.

"Wait for me," Ava said, going in after her sister.

Jack watched the pair scramble up to the walkway above the hide. In the main junction of the tree sat a pigeon loft, made from a dog crate. Inside were Twitch's two homing pigeons, Frazzle and Squeaker. Grabbing the knotted rope suspended between the walkway and the crow's nest, Tippi climbed, pulling herself up into the wooden barrel that was bolted around a tall, mast-like branch.

"There's a seat in here!" she called down to Ava. "Oooh, you can see for miles."

Jack went into the cabin that branched off left from the tepee. He moved the hessian sack of fat balls that they had made from lard and seeds, which they hung around the wood every week for hungry birds surviving the winter. Tara started stapling sheets of white paper to the back wall to create a backdrop for their case map. Taking the freezer bag of monkey-nut shells, Jack pinned it to the papered wall. It was their first clue.

Ozuru settled down at the table – a board on top of two milk crates – with a large sheet of paper, a ruler and a pencil. He began drawing the crime timeline.

"Is Twitch all right?" Terry was standing at the birdwatching window that overlooked the pond. Twitch was outside, staring across the water. "Is he still thinking about the peregrine falcons?"

"Yeah, but, also, we haven't found his binoculars," Jack said.

There was a thud. Ava lurched through the cabin doorway, her face alert, her voice a whisper. "There's someone spying on us."

"What! Who?" Jack whispered back.

"Don't know. Tippi spotted them through her binoculars. Someone in a yellow jumper is crouched in the trees along the edge of the pond, and they have binoculars."

"It might be the egg thief!" Terry said in an excited voice. "Perhaps they suspect we're on to them and are watching to see what we're going to do next."

Ava gave him a wry look. "We haven't got a clue who the egg thief is yet."

"We've one clue." Terry pointed at the nut shells. "And they don't know that we don't know who they are, do they?"

Ava rolled her eyes.

"What should we do?" Ozuru asked Jack.

"Find out who they are and what they are doing."

"We'll do it," Terry said, turning to Ozuru. "Right?"

"Did Tippi say if they were big?" Ozuru asked Ava.

"Come on." Terry grabbed his arm and they scampered out of the hide.

Jack looked down at Ozuru's timeline and Ava came to stand beside him.

"Twitch says the thief will be knowledgeable about birds," Tara said, joining them.

"They will be," Twitch's voice came from the doorway. "I've been thinking about what you asked, about the birds protecting their nest. They almost definitely would have attacked. Jack, remember that seagull that stole your doughnut? The falcons will have dropped down from above the thief, using their talons to attack. Even if they were wearing a helmet, the thief would have to fend the birds off with their hands and arms."

"Which is why they'd need gloves," Ava looked at Jack.

"We need to keep a lookout for people with scratches on their heads and their hands or wrists," Twitch said, sitting down on a tree stump at the table. "But, I've been thinking. If the thief is still here, in Briddvale, they will keep stealing. I think the best way to protect birds' eggs and catch the thief is to set up a nest watch."

"How would we do that?" Ava asked.

"We can patrol the woods in the daytime, keeping an eye out for anyone acting suspiciously, looking interested in nests."

"What do we do if we see someone doing that?" Tara asked, looking nervous.

"Engage them in cheerful conversation. Make it clear that we've seen them," Twitch replied. "Which might put them off coming back."

"We could set up snares or booby traps around trees that we suspect might get targeted," Jack said, warming to this idea.

"I think we should make a note of every nest we see and keep a record of any eggs we spot. That way, if any are stolen, we'll know." Twitch pulled a crumpled map from his pocket. It was covered in numbers. "I made this map last year. It's of the bird boxes around the nature reserve. It shows their locations and numbers. We can check to see which ones have birds in."

"This is a good idea!" Jack said enthusiastically. "It will give us evidence if the thief strikes again, and if we witness them in action, boom, straight to jail they go."

"Nesting birds are nervous," Twitch said. "It's important no one gets too near a nest. Frightened adult birds can abandon their nests and the eggs inside it."

"We'll be super careful," Tara reassured him.

"If we're near nests, we can communicate with sign language, rather than having to talk," Jack suggested.

Tippi's face appeared at the doorway. "Terry and Ozuru are coming back. They've got a girl with them!"

To Jack's surprise, Terry and Ozuru brought a sheepish-looking Pippa Bettany into the hide. She peered about eagerly, greedily taking in every detail.

"Found her crouching in a clump of ferns, spying on us through her bins!" Terry said.

"I wasn't spying..." Pippa spluttered. "I was... I was..."

"Who are you?" Tippi peered curiously at the girl.

"Twitch's stalker," Jack replied. "She follows him everywhere."

"I don't!" Pippa's face flushed purple. She looked at the seven accusing faces and her lip wobbled. "I... I wanted..." She stalled, her mouth open. Abruptly, she pivoted, darted past Terry and disappeared out the door.

"She's fast!" Terry looked startled. "Shall I go after her?"

"No," Twitch replied. "Pippa's harmless, and we've got work to do."

"But as soon as we've caught the thief," Jack said, "we are building up the camouflage around the hide. If Pippa Bettany can find us, anyone can."

9

TWO BIRDS. ONE STONE.

Twitch signalled for everyone to gather round the table and sit down. Tara took out sandwiches and biscuits from her rucksack and handed them around as Twitch explained Project Nest Watch to Terry, Ozuru and Tippi. "If you do spot a nest, don't go near it. If we want a closer look, we can use binoculars or my camera. We don't want to lead predators, human or any other kind, to a vulnerable nest."

"And if we spot someone creeping about looking into nests," Ava said, "we'll challenge them."

"And tell the police," Tara added.

Raising his right hand, Jack drew his first two fingers together, tapping them twice against his thumb, making the sign for *bird*.

Everyone copied, and they launched into The Twitchers Oath.

"I do solemnly swear never to knowingly hurt a bird.
I will respect my feathered friends and help them when they are in need.
I will protect every bird, be it rare, endangered or common, and fight to conserve their habitats, or may crows peck out my eyes when I am dead.
For I am a Twitcher, now and for ever."

"If the egg thief is a competitor in the Canal Masters, they might be fishing right now," Jack said. "Which means the birds nesting closest to the canal are the ones most in danger. We should patrol there first."

"And interview anyone fishing," Ava suggested.

"Kill two birds with one stone," Terry added, and everyone winced.

"We'll patrol the canal side first," Twitch agreed, rising to his feet. "Let's go."

Hanging back, Twitch let Jack lead everyone out of the hide. He followed behind, scanning the tree canopy for nests. He wasn't the best detective when it came to human behaviour, but he was brilliant at detecting birds.

"Look," Ozuru said in a low voice. "A police officer."

Twitch recognized the female police officer whose lips he'd read on Passerine Pike. She had a bundle of lime-green flyers under her arm and a staple gun in her hand. She was walking away from the noticeboard beside the signpost. The Twitchers clamoured around it. In the middle of the usual notices about walks and the types of animals that could be spotted in the nature reserve was a lime-green flyer. It read:

WARNING!

BIRD EGG THIEVES OPERATING IN THIS AREA!

Protect your local wildlife. Be on the lookout for suspicious behaviour or people loitering near nests. If you see anything, please call the National Wildlife Crime Unit. Taking eggs from the nest of a wild bird is against the law and punishable with a custodial sentence.

A photocopied picture of a nest with eggs in it and a telephone number in bold were at the bottom of the page.

"Is that all they're doing?" Twitch was unimpressed. "Putting up a few flyers and relying on people to call the NWCU? By the time anyone got out here, the eggs and the thief would be gone."

"What else can they do?" Terry asked. "They can't

exactly hang around every tree in Briddvale in case a thief shows up."

Twitch's thoughts roiled and churned as they carried on up the footpath. That flyer wouldn't deter a thief who struck at night when there were no passers-by to stop them. He wracked his brains to think of a way to catch or track the egger. He thought they might use their phones as security cameras, but how would they know where to put them? Would they pick up images in the dark? What if they ran out of battery? No, cameras weren't the answer. He liked Jack's plan of setting up traps, but what kind of traps? And where? A bird thief could strike anywhere. Twitch drew blank after blank and kept returning to the thought that he needed to be out, patrolling the woods, protecting the birds at night. He knew this idea wouldn't go down well with the others.

Tippi's sudden squeal of pleasure shook him from his thoughts. "I found a nest!" she said, running towards him, pointing back at the hedgerow beside the kissing gate that led onto the towpath. "It's got eggs in it!" Her face was the definition of wonder. "They're blue!"

Using sign language, Twitch told the others to move on through the gate and up the towpath. When they'd gone, he took Tippi's hand, and the pair approached the hedgerow. She took him a couple of metres away from the gate and pointed to a spot in the thicket of unfurling citrus-green leaves.

"Do you see it?" Tippi signed.

"I see," Twitch signed back. Looking up, he spotted a pair of agitated birds circling. He pulled Tippi back so the birds above would see they weren't a threat. Lifting his long-lens camera, he snapped a series of close-up pictures of the nest.

"Let's go," he signed. When they were through the gate and a little way along the towpath, Twitch showed her the images on the screen at the back of the camera, zooming in on the nest.

"Ooh, look at the grasses and roots woven together, stuffed with moss." Tippi studied the screen. "It's so beautiful. What are those bits?"

"Lichens and animal hair."

Tippi pointed to the three delicate pale blue eggs spattered with reddish-brown. "What bird do they belong to?"

"Bullfinch," Twitch replied. "You wouldn't expect to see them laying eggs for at least a couple more weeks, but the weather is warm for this time of year."

"Are they rare?" Tippi asked, still staring at them.

"Not really. Pretty common." Twitch felt the

dragging sensation in his stomach that accompanied his worries about declining bird populations. "At least, they are for now. Well done, Tippi. You've spotted our first clutch!" She grew an inch taller. "We'll ask Ozuru to make a chart, mapping where nests with eggs are. Your bullfinch nest will be the first to go on it."

"I'm going to paint a picture of it when we get to Tara's."

"Good idea. Come on. We'd better catch up with the others." Down the towpath, Twitch saw them approaching a fisherman with a shaved head. He caught his breath as he recognized the man in the red shirt and black combats as the person he'd seen last night, sitting in the silver VW in Passerine Pike car park. The fisherman was standing at the edge of the canal, staring at the water as he cast his line.

Twitch heard Jack say, "Good afternoon, sir, are you taking part in the Canal Masters?"

"What's it to you?" The shaven-headed man didn't take his gaze off the water.

"Nothing, we were, er … just welcoming all the competitors to Briddvale," Jack said, and Twitch felt a grudging respect for his friend's ability to come out with utter nonsense under pressure.

"Right." The man turned to look at Jack, and Twitch

felt a lurch as he saw that above the man's left eyebrow was a nasty cut. "Consider me welcomed."

"How did you cut yourself?" Ava asked.

"What?"

"Above your eye." She gestured.

"Oh. That. It was a bramble."

Twitch and Tippi joined the group and the man glanced at him. The hairs on the back of Twitch's neck lifted as he saw a flicker of recognition in the man's eyes.

"Where've you been?" Jack said. "We're just welcoming, er…" He gestured at the man. "Mr er…"

"Jed Butler," the man replied, looking hard at Twitch.

"We were taking photographs of a nest," Tippi told Jack proudly. "There is lichen and animal hair in it and the eggs are bullfinch eggs!"

"Bullfinch eggs?" The fisherman frowned and turned away. "Bit early, isn't it?"

Twitch stiffened at this display of knowledge from the fisherman. "It's been a pretty mild winter," he replied hesitantly.

"You're not wrong." The fisherman looked back at the water. "Where was the nest?"

"Oh, in Aves Wood," Twitch lied. "Near the bird-feeding station."

Jack's hands were moving. He was signing. *"Is he the man you saw on Thursday?"*

Twitch gave a little shake of his head and signed, *"Friday."*

"Ask him something," Jack pressed.

"Do you like watching birds?" Twitch said.

"Started fishing to have something to do whilst watching birds." The man reeled in an empty hook and Twitch noticed how his muscles bulged. Jed Butler was strong enough to climb rocks and trees with ease. "Now I know the fish better, birdwatching's something I do whilst fishing." He smiled. His teeth were stained yellow from smoking. "What did you do to get that nasty scratch on the back of your hand?"

"Hawthorn tree," Twitch replied, not liking the way the prickly man was looking at him.

"Hmm, they can be vicious." He fed a bit of bait onto his fishing hook. "Like birds' eggs, do you?"

Twitch was shocked by the question and spluttered out an answer. "I like the chicks that come out of them." He glanced at Jack, whose eyes were wide.

"Me too." Jed Butler cast his hook. It made a delicate splash as it hit the water. "Now, you've done your welcoming. Get away and let me fish."

10

DANDELION MAN

Twitch couldn't stop thinking about Jed Butler for the rest of the afternoon. He felt certain they had just met an egg thief. Jack kept telling him that he had to keep an open mind to be a good detective, but he knew in his gut that Jed was guilty. They didn't encounter any other competitors along the canal and the sky had become overcast and was threatening to rain.

At five o'clock, Tara announced that she was taking Ava and Tippi home to unpack and eat some food. Terry and Ozuru decided to go with them.

"Are you going to go home?" Jack asked Twitch as they waved goodbye.

"In a bit. I need to go back to the hide and let out Frazzle and Squeaker."

As he followed Jack through the car park to their bikes, Twitch saw a wiry man with a thatch of straw-coloured hair come out of Aves Wood carrying a spade and what looked like a carrier bag of soil. His chest tightened around his heart in recognition. He pinched Jack's arm and signed, *"That's him!"* The stranger lolloped past them, oblivious to the staring boys. *"That's the man I saw on the hill on Thursday night!"*

"Let's follow him!" Jack signed back.

Sauntering casually but quickly over to their bikes, Jack unlocked them. Twitch kept his eyes on the wiry man who was now crossing Crowther Bridge. Was *this* the egg thief, not Jed Butler? There was definitely something odd about him. Twitch recalled being up the pike and the rain coming down. He had hurried home, but this man had stayed out on the hillside unconcerned by the downpour.

Side by side, Twitch and Jack wheeled their bikes over the bridge, keeping a safe distance between them and their quarry.

"What if he's got a car?" Twitch whispered.

"We'll pedal fast," Jack replied and Twitch could hear the excitement in his voice.

When they got to the Briddvale Road, the wiry man was standing beside a battered blue moped. There was a piece of rope tied between the neck of his spade and the handle. He pulled this over his head, so the spade sat diagonally across his back. The top box bolted to the rear of the vehicle was open. From it, he took a bulbous yellow helmet, putting it on, and dropped his carrier bag of soil inside. Taking a pair of goggles from his coat pocket, he pulled them over his helmet, arranging them over his eyes. Straddling the moped, the wiry man lifted the kickstand with his foot and manoeuvred the vehicle around. He turned the key in the ignition and the engine coughed a few farting growls. Sticking out his arm to indicate he was moving off, even though there was no traffic on the road, he pootled away.

"We'll be able to keep up with him, easy," Jack said, pushing his bike forward up the little incline onto the road.

The two boys pedalled furiously to close the distance between them and the suspect, then slowed down.

"We need to keep him in our sights," Jack said. "But we don't want to get so close that he notices us."

"Why do you think he's got a spade and soil?" Twitch asked.

"Maybe he was burying his stolen eggs! So that he isn't caught with them."

"That doesn't explain why he's carrying around a bag of soil."

"Or why he looks like a giant dandelion."

Twitch laughed. He'd thought the same thing when the man had pulled on his yellow helmet.

The suspect exited the Briddvale Road, heading towards Passerine Pike, but then turned into Patchem's farm. The boys shot past the driveway and hit their brakes, skidding to a stop.

Twitch could hear the *putt-putt-putt* of the moped disappearing down the drive. "He's staying at the campsite!"

"Let's hide our bikes and go see."

Twitch jumped off his bike, wheeling it backwards and letting it fall against the hedgerow. The bush swallowed the bike, catching its handlebars and saddle, stopping it from hitting the ground. Only the tyres could be seen poking out the bottom of the hedge. Jack did the same.

Twitch knew Patchem's farm well. His grandparents used to bring him here when he was little to see the farm animals. Here, chickens strutted about, roaming where their claws took them, and you could pick your own raspberries and strawberries in early summer.

As they walked up the drive, Jack bent low, looking about furtively.

"You don't need to creep about." Twitch suppressed a smile. "Plenty of people come here. We can say we're visiting the shop." He pointed at the barn with a big white board saying Patchem's Farm Shop on it.

"Cool." Jack straightened up, putting his hands in his pockets, trying to look relaxed.

"The campsite is down there, past the shop, in Skeleton Tree Field."

"Skeleton Tree Field?"

"The camping field. It has a tree right in the middle that is as white as bone. It's bare of leaves or any sign of life. Mum told me that when she was little it was struck by lightning. It's so pale that under a full moon it almost glows. It doesn't seem to rot or decay in the way other trees do. It's super spooky…"

"There's a skeleton tree in Briddvale and you're only just telling me? This I need to see!"

At the end of the track was a field containing a handful of colourful tents. Rising from the middle of it was an eerie white skeletal tree. Jack let out a low whistle.

"Whoa! All it needs is a dead pirate hanging from a noose, a few corvids, and it would be perfect!"

"There's something wrong with you, you know that?"

"Look!" Jack nudged Twitch's arm.

Beyond the gate was a gravel patch. Their suspect's

moped was parked in it. Next to it was a silver VW.

"That's Jed Butler's car!" Twitch exclaimed in a whisper. "Do you think he's staying here too?" He suddenly felt conspicuous and looked around.

"I can't see him, or the human dandelion. They must be in their tents. Come on, let's look in—" He broke off.

Twitch heard a woman's voice and a man chortling. A glance behind them, down the track, showed Mr and Mrs Drake approaching. Merle Drake was carrying his tackle box. Evelyn Drake was wearing her cheerful burgundy hat and leaning on a walking stick. The two camping chairs were slung over her shoulder in their cases.

"Quick," Jack said, grabbing the top of the metal gate and stepping a foot up. He was over in a flash. Twitch was right behind him. They dashed to the vehicles, ducking down behind Jed Butler's silver car, and watched Mr and Mrs Drake open the gate and make their way to the largest tent in the field. It was forest green, with a porch.

"Mr Patchem's doing well out of this fishing competition," Twitch whispered.

"Bit mean of Mr Drake to make his wife carry the chairs if she needs a walking stick," Jack replied as Mrs Drake dropped the chairs to the ground. They watched her unzip the door of the tent and roll it up, fixing it open with a strap, as her husband set down his tackle box beside a camping stove on a table.

"Time to hunt for clues." Jack pointed to the interior of Jed Butler's car. "Have you got your notebook?" Twitch pulled it from his pocket. "Good. Look through the windows. Write a list of everything you can see, even if it seems unimportant."

"What are you going to do?"

"The moped," Jack said, pulling out his own notebook.

The pair worked silently for five minutes.

Twitch faithfully wrote down the sweet wrappers and disposable coffee cups he saw in the front of the car. On the back seat was a crumpled fleece. His eyes dropped to the footwell and he stiffened. "Jack," he hissed. "Come see."

In a heartbeat, Jack was there. Twitch pointed at the mess of rope, cord, webbing and carabiners. "That is a rock-climbing harness!"

They exchanged a wide-eyed look.

"Evidence!" Jack exhaled the word with reverence.

"I told you it was Jed Butler." Twitch dropped to the ground, slid off his rucksack and withdrew his camera. He removed the long lens, screwing on a short one, and took a series of pictures of the inside of the car, concentrating on getting the climbing gear in focus.

"Look!" Jack pointed at a book poking out from underneath the fleece on the back seat. "It's the SAS Survival Handbook!"

Twitch took a picture of it.

"I think you might be right about Jed," Jack conceded.

"Did you find anything in the moped?"

"I didn't see anything that could be a clue. The box at the back just has that carrier bag of mud in it."

"Did you lift the seat? There's usually storage under the saddle."

Jack returned to the moped. Twitch watched him wrestle with a catch under the seat and then it popped up. He peered inside. His eyes widened as he lifted out a half-eaten bag of monkey nuts. "You said you saw Dandelion Man on the path above the car park when it started to rain?" Twitch nodded. "This means that after it stopped raining, he went up the hill and sat down on that rock near the nest."

Twitch took a photo of Jack holding the bag of nuts.

"Do you think Dandelion Man and Jed could be in it together?" Jack asked.

"People don't share egg collections." Twitch shook

his head. "Is there anything else in there?"

"Just some old CDs of classical music."

"Henley!" Mrs Drake's voice called out. "Would you like to join us for a cup of tea, dear?"

Jack let the seat fall shut as they both dropped to the ground.

"Oh my goodness," Jack groaned. "Do you smell that? Someone's frying bacon. It's making me hungry."

"I know you know I'm vegetarian," Twitch said, peering over the bonnet of Jed Butler's car.

"Yeah, but, bacon. Doesn't that smell get to you? I thought even vegetarians liked crispy bacon."

"Not me." Twitch watched the dandelion man stride across the field to the Drakes' tent, where he accepted a tin mug from Mrs Drake. "Pigs' butt cheeks have never made me hungry." Mr Drake was standing at the camping stove, cooking. Twitch guessed that was where the fried bacon smell was coming from. He strained his ears but couldn't hear what they were saying. However, he did hear Jack's stomach growl. "Dandelion Man's name is Henley," he whispered, nodding at Jack's pad. "Write that down."

Jack was licking his lips as he scribbled. "I need to eat. I'm starving."

"We're on a stakeout," Twitch chided.

"Oh, steak. I'd love steak and chips right now, with extra ketchup." Jack saw the way Twitch was looking at him and held up his notebook. "Look, we've done brilliantly today. We've learned loads; we have a list of named suspects."

"Who is on the list?"

"Jed Butler, obviously, Henley Dandelion, and Mr and Mrs Drake because they're doing the fishing competition, and … er … yeah. That's it, but that's four more people than we had this morning." He covered his stomach as it grumbled again. "I've got to go home and eat. I can't think straight."

"Yeah, OK," Twitch said, realizing Jack was right.

"The good thing is that the egg thief is probably one of the people in this campsite; so no birds are in danger right now," Jack reasoned.

Twitch was about to remind Jack of his own advice that they should keep an open mind about who the thief was, but Jack was already walking towards the gate.

"Come on. Let's go home," Jack said, over his shoulder.

"Do you think we should tell Constable Greenwood about Jed Butler?" Twitch asked, as they clambered over the gate and headed back down the track to their bikes.

"Not yet. We don't have evidence that could lead to an arrest. We can't just pin it on the first person who seems guilty. It could be Henley. We know he was on Passerine Pike on Thursday and the monkey nuts prove he went up the hill."

"I suppose," Twitch said. "Hey, can I borrow your microphone tonight? You can have it back tomorrow morning. I want to try something."

"Sure. Don't suppose you've got any sweets or anything I could eat right now, do you? It feels like my stomach is eating itself in here." He patted his belly.

"Sorry. No."

When they reached their bikes, Jack fished the microphone out of his rucksack and shoved it into Twitch's hands, eager to get on his bike and find food.

"I was thinking—" Twitch started to say.

"See you in the morning," Jack called out as he cycled away.

Twitch looked down at the microphone. He wanted to know just how far it could reach. Tonight, he would find out. He was going to use it to guard the birds of Aves Wood.

11

EGG AND SPOON

Jack almost skipped to the hide the next morning. The birds were singing riotously in the trees, reflecting his mood. The woods looked magical dressed in a fine layer of frost. Last night, after dinner, he'd spent the evening working on the case, building a picture of the events of last Thursday night. He had two main suspects, Jed and Henley, and he felt certain that today they would make a breakthrough. What they needed was a witness or a good piece of evidence. It occurred to him that the strongest evidence would be the stolen eggs. He wondered where they might be. Had Henley buried them?

The hide door was closed when he reached it. He yanked on the hanger and went inside. To his surprise he saw a roll mat, sleeping bag and pillow in the tent room that branched off the right side of the tepee.

"Twitch?" Jack called out. There was no reply.

He found the remnants of Twitch's dinner on the table in the cabin: a water flask, greaseproof paper that must've wrapped his sandwiches, and orange peel. Climbing the ladder, Jack greeted Frazzle and Squeaker, who were still in the pigeon loft and probably kept Twitch company last night. Grabbing the knotted rope, he pulled himself up into the crow's nest, where he was astonished to find his parabolic microphone rigged up and strapped to the branch that the crow's nest was built around. He pulled the headphones over his ears. A wave of birdsong broke over him.

Sitting down heavily, Jack suddenly felt he'd let Twitch down. He should've known his friend would've wanted to patrol and protect the birds in Aves Wood last night. It was totally the kind of thing Twitch would do. But he'd been so desperate to eat that he hadn't thought about what Twitch was doing. He'd known his friend had to go back to the hide and let out the pigeons, but in his hurry to find food he'd forgotten. He clapped his hand to his forehead. He wished Twitch had said something.

Through the headphones, he became aware of the sound of rustling undergrowth and footsteps. He heard a stick snap and the whoosh of a leafy branch pinging back into position. Standing up, he lifted his binoculars and scanned the woods. He spotted an unfamiliar white bird on the west shore of the pond. He still had so much to learn before he was half the birder Twitch was. Further to the right he saw his headstrong friend walking through the trees. Jack waited until Twitch looked up and then waved. He saw Twitch speed up, and Jack clambered down to the walkway.

"Jack!" Twitch called out, looking up through the ladder-hole, his expression guilty. "Look, I know what you're going to say…"

"You camped out in the hide!" Jack blurted out. "Without me!"

"I didn't know I was definitely going to. It's just, I had to come back to let the pigeons out and I wanted to see if your microphone could pick up people coming and going in the woods." He shrugged. "Once I was here, I kept thinking about Jed Butler coming to steal eggs and … well, I had to stay, to protect the birds…" Twitch dropped his head. "Sorry."

"Next time, we do it together," Jack huffed.

"OK." Twitch gave him a meek smile. "It would've been more fun if you'd been here," he admitted, picking up a plastic tub of birdseed and shinning up the ladder. "And even though it was freezing, I kept falling asleep."

Twitch opened the door to the pigeon loft. "Hey, Frazzle. Morning, Squeaker." He filled their empty bowl. "Grub's up."

"Weren't you scared on your own?" Jack asked, knowing he would've been.

Twitch shook his head as the dazzle-eyed, scruffy Frazzle fluttered down from his nesting box to the silver dish. "Right here, in the hide, is where I feel most at home in all the world."

"Last night, I worked on the case," Jack told him, sitting down on the walkway, facing the pond. "Both Jed Butler and Henley are strong suspects."

"It's Jed," Twitch said, closing the coop door and sitting down beside him. "I know it. The way he looked at me when he asked me that question about eggs…" He shivered.

"The best evidence we could find would be the stolen eggs. If we discovered them in his tent or his car, the police would have to arrest him."

The two boys sat in silence for a moment, looking out over the shimmering mercury-grey water of the pond, thinking about Jed Butler.

"I'm sorry I didn't tell you I was going to camp here," Twitch said softly.

"Did you see anyone last night?"

"No. But your microphone is brilliant. I made some recordings of nocturnal birds. I even heard a toad singing." Twitch glanced sideways at him to see if he was still cross. "I thought about our nest watch patrol and I've realized how impossible it is to guard all the nests. Birds don't just nest in trees; they nest on the ground, and in reeds. It's the wrong way to protect them. Your microphone means we can listen out for humans. Tracking any human who comes into the wood at night is much easier than trying to guard every nest. I was thinking we could tie a long blade of grass around each of the three entrance gates, which will snap if someone uses them. A regular patrol will alert us to someone being in the woods. And humans are noisy. We can use your microphone to find them."

As Twitch was talking, Jack saw the big white bird again and lifted his binoculars to get a better look.

"Jack, are you listening to me?" There was a hint of irritation in Twitch's voice.

"Sorry." Jack passed his binoculars to Twitch, remembering his friend had lost his. "It's just there's a white bird out there and I have no idea what it is."

"What?" Twitch took the binoculars.

"I think it's a wader?"

"It can't be!" Twitch whispered as he focused

103

the lenses. "Oh, Jack!" He sprang up, thrusting the binoculars back into Jack's hands, and raced to the ladder. "Quick! Come on!"

Taken aback, Jack followed Twitch, who grabbed his camera as he dashed out of the hide. Jack sprinted after him, along the marshy shore of the pond. A frenzy seemed to have overtaken his friend, who was trying to screw the long lens onto his camera as he ran. Jack panned across the water with his binoculars and pointed. "There it is."

The elegant white waterbird was stalking through the shallows of the pond on dark spindly legs. It had an unusual black beak shaped like two spoons, or spatulas. An ocean-blue dragonfly flitted past. The spoons opened and clapped together, catching it. Jack saw a dash of yellow on the breast feathers and bill tip of the bird as it swallowed the unfortunate dragonfly.

"I don't believe it!" Twitch said as he looked through his camera. "It's a lifer, Jack! A new bird for our lists."

"It's the weirdest-looking duck I've ever seen," Jack said. "Look at its beak!"

"Do you know what it is?" Twitch's eyes were shining.

"No. Shall I get the field guide?"

"Jack. It's a spoonbill! I've never seen one before. Ever! We've never had one in Aves Wood!"

Jack grinned at the wonder on his friend's face. He lifted his binoculars. "A spoonbill," he echoed. "I can see how it got that name." Then a second spoonbill came stalking out of the reeds. "Twitch! There are two of them!"

Twitch jerked the camera up to his eye. "A pair of spoonbills!" His voice was an excited squeak. "The second one is smaller with a slightly shorter beak. Do you see? I think that's a female."

They stumbled along the shoreline with their eyes glued to their lenses. Jack's heart was thumping against his ribcage as he watched the two birds fishing for their breakfast in the water with their comedic beaks.

"This is so super mega rare!" Twitch told Jack as they found a seat on the knotty roots of a tree, behind a thicket of mugwort. They watched the male bird present sticks to the female. Twitch took photographs.

"Do you think they'll stay?" Jack asked.

"I don't know. I can't believe they've come here," Twitch whispered. "They will've migrated from Egypt or Sudan, all the way to Briddvale!" He shook his head in amazement. "Do you know, spoonbills used to breed in this country, like, in medieval times, but they stopped hundreds of years ago. Then, about ten years ago, a small number nested on the coast. It was big birding news. And now they're here in Aves Wood!" He was unable to take his eyes off the birds.

"What are they doing?"

"I guess they're looking for somewhere to build a nest. I think the female spoonbill usually makes it. The male gathers the building materials."

"Is that why he keeps giving her sticks?"

"It's unusual to see a pair nesting on their own. Spoonbills normally nest in colonies."

"Perhaps if they nest here, it will build a colony. Imagine a whole colony of spoonbills!" Jack smiled at this idea. "Baby spoonbills must be cute, with their little clapping beaks…"

A horrible thought landed in Jack's head at the same time as Twitch's expression became grave.

"Will the thief want spoonbill eggs?" Jack asked, already knowing the answer.

"If there is a spoonbill nest, we have to find it and protect it!"

12

EGG ON FACE

Jack had to trot to keep up with Twitch as he marched back to the hide. Tara waved to them from the walkway and Jack waved back, but Twitch didn't notice.

"We're going to have to keep a permanent watch on the shores of the pond," Twitch told him.

"There are no paths around the pond," Jack pointed out. "Anyone trying to find the nest will end up in the freezing water."

"That won't stop Jed Butler. It's part of the challenge for eggers. The more difficult the nest is to reach, the more determined they are to reach it, like an extreme sport."

Jack had an idea. "What if we borrowed Ozuru's boat?" he suggested. "We could use it to patrol the water and guard the nest from the middle of the pond."

"That's a brilliant idea!" Twitch gave him a look of admiration that made Jack glow.

Following Twitch into the hide, Jack saw that everyone had arrived while they'd been watching the spoonbills, except Terry.

"Hooray!" Tippi bounded up to him. "You're both here."

Ozuru was sitting at the table, working on his crime timeline. Ava was standing with her back to him and her hands on her hips, studying the crime wall. "Oh good, you're back," she said without turning around. "What does this mean?" She pointed to a scrap of paper that said: *climbing equipment found in Jed Butler's car.*

"I put that there last night," Twitch told Jack.

"Twitch and I have lots to tell you," Jack said, sitting down at the table and pulling out his notebook.

"Wait for me." Tara shinned down the ladder to join them.

"After you went home," Jack told them, "Twitch spotted the man he saw up the pike on Thursday. We followed him."

"No way!" Ozuru exclaimed.

"What's all the excitement about?" came Terry's sleepy voice, followed by his toothpaste-stained face and unbrushed curly hair. He was wearing a faded shirt over a long-sleeved T-shirt.

"Did you fall out of bed into your clothes?" Ava asked.

"Maybe." Terry blinked, wiping sleep from his eyes. He handed a carrier bag to Ava. She opened it. It had her purple tracksuit in it. "I washed it."

"Your shirt," Tara pointed. "It's buttoned up wrong."

"It's on purpose." Terry looked down and shrugged.

"It's cool." Tippi giggled. "I hope you haven't solved the crime without me," he said, sitting down at the table.

"They were about to tell us," Ava said.

"Well" – Jack took a second to enjoy the anticipation on everyone's faces – "let's just say, there is a lot going on at Patchem's farm right now." Using his notebook as a prompt, he told the others about following Henley to the farm. Twitch showed them the photographs he'd taken of the climbing equipment in Jed Butler's car.

"Who are our main suspects?" Tara asked, pen in hand.

"Jed Butler is our number one suspect." Jack looked at Twitch, who nodded in agreement. "Henley is second, then Mr and Mrs Drake because they're from out of town, and Pippa Bettany."

"Pippa?" Twitch blinked.

"You saw her on the pike on Friday," Jack reminded

him. "She was spying on us yesterday. She fits the profile in everything but age."

"She's a bit young to be out on her own after dark," Twitch said.

"She's the same age as me," Tippi said.

"Would you go up the pike on your own, in the dark?" Ava asked pointedly.

"Maybe." Tippi folded her arms. "You don't know."

"There's other news," Twitch said. "This morning, Jack and I spotted a pair of spoonbills in the shallow waters round the pond. I think they might be nesting."

"I love spoonbills!" Tippi exclaimed. "They have such funny beaks." She stuck out her chin and clapped her lips together.

"Spoonbills?" Tara looked astonished. "In Aves Wood?"

"Are you sure they weren't pale herons?" Terry looked sceptical.

"They're rare!" Ozuru looked stunned.

"How do you know they're nesting?" Ava asked.

"The male bird was gathering nesting materials," Twitch replied.

"Where there is a nest," Tara said, looking at the case wall, "there'll be eggs."

"Ozuru," Jack said, remembering his earlier idea. "Twitch and I were wondering if your dad might lend us your dinghy, to keep watch over the nests at the water's edge."

"We can go and ask him. Dad's fishing today," Ozuru replied. "The Canal Masters starts tomorrow. All the contestants will be practising today."

"Then that's where we should be." Jack stood up.

"If we see this Henley person, we can interrogate him," Ava said.

"In a way that doesn't alert him to the fact he's being interrogated," Jack replied.

Ava lifted an eyebrow. "I'm not an idiot."

"No. Of course not." Jack felt himself blush.

"Let's go!" Tippi yelled.

"The early worm catches the fish, as they say." Ozuru got to his feet.

"I'm not sure they do say that," Terry grumbled.

Taking the most direct route, through the trees to a break in the hedgerow onto the towpath, Ava led the way, with Ozuru and Terry almost jogging to keep pace. Twitch paused in the place where they'd heard the nightingale the previous day, looking for a nest, and Jack stayed with him. "See anything?"

Twitch shook his head.

"Maybe the nightingale's calls weren't answered," Jack said.

Twitch put a hand on his arm and signed the word, "*Listen*."

"*I hear nothing*," Jack signed back after a minute.

"*Exactly*," Twitch replied. "*Where is the birdsong?*" He tilted his head. "*Something has scared them.*"

A thrill raced up Jack's spine as they proceeded cautiously to the gap in the hedgerow through which the others had marched. What had frightened the birds away?

Jack saw Ozuru, with Tippi beside him, furthest down the towpath. Terry was right behind them, followed by Tara talking to Ava. The ivy-choked hedgerow beside Ozuru suddenly moved and lurched forward. Two branches of ivy reached out, grabbing at Tippi, who let out a terrified scream. Yanking herself away from the plant, she collided with Terry, who shrieked, windmilling his arms frantically as he lost his balance and toppled backwards into the canal. There was an almighty splash as he hit the water.

Pam appeared from nowhere, holding her microphone. "Wham! Bam! Pranked by Pam!"

Jack watched the ivy-clad figure lift the green stocking covering his face. It was Clem. He was pointing the camera at Pam, as Terry splashed around in the water behind her.

"Help! I can't swim!" Terry wailed, panicking and splashing with his flailing arms. "I'm drowning!"

"Put your feet down," Ozuru called out. "The canal isn't deep here."

Jack watched as Terry found the bottom with his feet and stood up. He had to suppress a smile. The water only came up to Terry's thighs.

"You bully!" Tippi shouted at Clem, kicking him in the shins hard.

Clem yelped and dropped the phone.

Jack turned to Twitch in amazement. "You knew they were waiting here!"

"No. I knew something had scared the birds away." He pointed to the sky and the wheeling birds.

"But still, you wouldn't have been pranked by Pam."

"Probably not." Twitch acknowledged with a little smile.

Jack shook his head in wonder. "I wish I could see the things you do."

"Come on." Twitch nudged him. "Let's go help poor Terry."

With encouragement from Ozuru and Ava, Terry was climbing up a slippery, algae-covered metal ladder at the side of the canal. Straggles of green weed were stuck to him. He was soaked to the skin.

"Uh-oh!" Pam said to the camera as Terry stomped angrily towards her. "It looks like the swamp thing doesn't have a sense of humour!"

Terry roared, running forward, opening his arms and grabbing Pam around the middle. She squealed as he lifted her off her feet, trying to carry her to the canal's edge. Pam, who didn't want a dunking, struggled violently. She kicked at Terry and he collapsed. They ended up in a tangle on the ground. Pam sat on him and started viciously poking his chest, as if typing hard on a keyboard.

"No!" Terry cried out, half laughing, half yelping in pain. "Stop!"

"Nasty" – *poke* – "dirty" – *poke* – "wet" – *poke* – "swamp thing," Pam crowed. "You've been defeated by a girl!"

Turning to Clem's camera, Pam flicked her hair away from her face, flexed her arm muscle and gave it a dazzling smile.

13

NEST EGGS

Twitch heard a shout. A little way up the towpath, he saw a rotund fisherman with a purple face getting out of his camping chair. "Will you lot keep it down! You're scaring the fish!"

Clem yanked Pam to her feet. His ivy costume rustled as they ran away.

"We're sorry, sir. We didn't mean to disturb you," Ozuru said, hurrying forward.

"It's not our fault." Ava's chin rose defiantly. "They pranked us!"

"That boy scared me," Tippi explained.

"Those idiots have been trying that trick on every passer-by for the last hour." The burly man grunted, sinking back into his seat. "You're the first to fall for it."

"We wouldn't have frightened the fish on purpose," Ozuru said apologetically. "Are you taking part in the

Canal Masters tomorrow?" The man nodded and Ozuru glanced at Jack. "Do you mind me asking your name, sir? My father is interested in who his competitors will be."

"What's your dad's name?" the fisherman asked, suspicious of Ozuru's question.

"Dr Sawa, Bolin Sawa."

"Never heard of him. How do you rate his chances?"

"Dad's a doctor," Ozuru said. "It's hard work. He fishes for the peace and to stop being a doctor for a bit." He paused, looking guilty as he said, "I'm not sure he's a very good fisherman. He doesn't catch much."

"Is he a good doctor?" the fisherman asked.

"Oh yes." Ozuru nodded. "Very good."

"That's much more important." The man smiled and Twitch was relieved to see that he wasn't angry. "My name's Phil Gordon. You tell your dad, he's up against one of the best anglers in the country." He winked and turned back to his rods. "I wish him the best of luck."

"Phil Gordon!" Jack said, sounding impressed. "Wow. It's an honour to meet you, sir." He reached out a hand and the fisherman shook it. "Are you staying in Briddvale?"

"Yes, at the Sozzled Stork. Good pub that."

"Did you arrive today?" Ava asked.

"Been down since Thursday. Trying out the different sections of canal. Never know what peg you'll draw."

"Do you know Jed Butler?" Twitch stepped forward. "He's taking part in the competition too. We met him yesterday."

"Not well. I've seen him at other tournaments." Phil Gordon lowered his voice. "He's not much competition. Easily distracted."

"Probably because he's a birdwatcher at heart," Twitch said, leadingly.

"Jed does like birds," Phil agreed. "Spent an evening in a pub with him once. He went on and on about the pear shape of guillemots' eggs stopping them from rolling off cliff edges." He shook his head. "Pity he doesn't learn more about fish."

Twitch shot Jack a triumphant glance.

"Do you know Henley?" Jack asked.

"That loon!" Phil laughed. "Everyone knows Henley Brandy. He's angling's mad inventor."

"Does he like birds?" Twitch asked.

"No idea." Phil shrugged. "But he's certainly crazy about fish. And speaking of fish…" He looked meaningfully at his fishing rod.

"We'll let you get back to it," Twitch said.

"It has been nice talking with you, Mr Gordon,"

Ozuru said. "Good luck in the competition tomorrow."

"Luck?" Phil said, leaning forward whilst pulling his rod back and speedily winding the reel. "I don't need luck."

A silver fish, about twenty centimetres long, came dancing out of the water, like a puppet on a string. Twitch watched in amazed silence as Phil Gordon got up, grabbed the handle of a large net sitting in the water and guided the fish into it. Kneeling down, he swiftly removed the hook. The net contained other fish that Phil had already caught. Twitch stared at them. He couldn't help feeling sorry for them. He wondered if the hook hurt.

"Come on." Ozuru pulled his arm, as the others moved along the towpath.

"Are you all right?" Twitch asked Terry, who was shivering.

"Do I look all right?" Terry looked down at his sodden, squelching, dripping body. "I'm wet and freezing!" He threw his hands out in an exasperated gesture and water flew from his fingertips. "Bother Pam and her stupid pranks. I'm going to have to go home and change!" He looked miserable. "I'll miss all the detecting."

"Oh, Terry," Tara said softly. "Do you want us to wait for you?"

"We can't," Jack said. "We need to solve this case as quickly as possible."

"It's fine," Terry sighed. "Go on without me. I'll catch up to you when I can."

"Or," Ava said, "you could nip back to the hide and put on my purple tracksuit?"

Hope ignited in Terry's eyes. "It would be quicker than going all the way home."

"There's a small towel in my rucksack," Twitch told him.

"I'll be back before you know it." Terry spun around and pelted away.

"That's two days in a row Pam has pranked Terry," Tara said.

"Tippi, your scream was epic," Jack said to her as they walked on. "It was like a girl from a horror movie. You know, when she comes face to face with a werewolf or Count Dracula!"

"Except it was Clem dressed in a leotard stuck with bits of ivy," Twitch said, and suddenly everyone was laughing.

"Oh!" Ava gasped. "What about when Terry thought he was drowning!" She held her sides as she laughed. "And Ozuru told him to stand up!"

"And then Pam beat him up!" Tippi added, giggling.

"Poor Terry!" Tara said, tears of laughter in her eyes.

"I think he did it on purpose so that he got to wear

your purple tracksuit again," Jack said, hooting.

They were still laughing when they reached the next lock and Twitch heard a distant voice calling out his name. He stopped, looking back along the canal. "Is that Terry?"

"Twitch!" Terry was sprinting back towards them, spray flying. "The nest!" he wheezed. "It's empty!"

"Which nest?" Twitch's heartbeat thumped in his ears.

"Bullfinch," Terry gasped. "The one Tippi found yesterday. I went through the gate…"

"The beautiful blue eggs?" Tippi's voice was a whisper.

Terry looked at her mournfully. "Gone!"

"All of them?"

He nodded. "Stolen!"

"Could it have been a predator?" Jack asked Twitch.

"Possibly." Twitch thought about the position of the nest. It was well hidden, in the thick of the hedgerow, over a metre off the ground. "Lots of animals eat birds' eggs. Foxes do, but they go for bigger eggs, like hens' or pheasants'. Rats and squirrels make holes in an egg and eat it there rather than move it. There'd be shells left in the nest or on the ground. Same with magpies or corvids. They'd stick their beak in and eat. But, if the nest is totally empty..." He felt a twisting in his stomach. "It seems our thief has struck again."

"It's right by the canal," Tara said. "Where everybody is fishing."

"Jed Butler asked me where the nest was," Twitch said, looking at Jack.

"But you told him it was in Aves Wood," Jack reminded him.

"A skilled birdwatcher on the lookout for bullfinches would easily find that nest," Twitch said, wishing Tippi hadn't mentioned the nest in front of the man. His heart sank. How many other nests had been robbed that they didn't know about? Would never know about. He'd tried to stay up all night to guard the birds, but he knew he'd fallen asleep at least twice while listening through the microphone. And despite patrolling the paths several times, he'd seen nothing. Jed Butler had beaten him.

"I will add this theft to the timeline," Ozuru said sombrely.

"Poor bullfinches." Tippi's eyes were brimming with tears.

"I think we should add Pam to our suspect list," Terry said. "She was hiding right by it."

"Terry," Tara said with a reprimanding tone, "you

know as well as I do that Pam would never climb into a hedgerow."

"Not unless there was a famous person hiding in it," Ozuru agreed.

Twitch felt as upset as Tippi looked. He put his arm around her shoulders. "We *will* get the person who is doing this," he told her, "and we *will* stop them." She looked up, her eyes showing her utter belief in him. He felt like a horrible fraud. The thief had targeted the bullfinches and, despite his best efforts, Twitch had failed to catch him.

UNDER HIS WING

Twitch spent the evening poring over his bird books, trying to keep his eyes open and learn everything he could about spoonbills and their nests. After the initial excitement of discovering the birds, the day had gone downhill. Pam's prank, followed by Terry's discovery about the bullfinch eggs had affected everyone's mood. They'd tried to talk to Jed Butler again but he'd told them to sling their hook and Henley Brandy was nowhere to be found. The only good things were that they'd added Phil Gordon's name to their suspect list and Ozuru's dad had said they could have the boat to patrol the pond. Twitch was so tired, after trying to stay awake all night, that Jack had insisted he go home, pointing out that he had to take care of his chickens and his mum would smell a rat if he didn't. After much discussion, Ozuru had gone to the police station to report the missing bullfinch eggs, and Jack and Terry had volunteered to camp in the hide tonight to do the night watch, promising Twitch that they would guard the spoonbills.

The next morning, despite sleeping soundly, Twitch was so weighed down with worry that his body felt as heavy as lead. He couldn't bear the thought of Jed Butler discovering the characterful white waders and destroying any chance of their having babies. He was desperate to get back to the birds and reassure himself that they were all right. He speedily threw his clothes on, fed the hens, released his pigeons, and jumped on his bike.

As he cycled, he came to the conclusion that he should search for the spoonbill nest on his own, before going to the hide. He didn't think the birds had been in Aves Wood long, a week at most. He would've seen them if they'd arrived before last weekend. Today was the first of April, which was early in the spoonbill nesting season, so it was unlikely there would be any eggs for Jed Butler to steal just yet. He knew Aves Wood better than he knew his own face and was certain he could find the nest without disturbing any birds or other wildlife. Nor would he fall foul of the marshy waterlogged land around the pond. His book on waders had said spoonbill nests were made with twigs and sticks, woven together with reeds or stems and lined with soft leaves and grass. It was hard to tell the exact size from the photographs, but it looked like the nest would be big. This, Twitch thought, should make it easy to spot. The tricky thing was that it could be anywhere. Spoonbills nested on the ground, in reeds, up in trees and in bushes. He was wondering where he might find the spoonbill nest when he heard a splash, a yelping honk, and a woman's voice cried out, "Shoo! Shoo! Away with you!"

Pulling on his brakes, Twitch came to a stop before Aves Lock and saw a woman on her knees. There was a burgundy hat on the towpath beside her. "Mrs Drake!" he exclaimed, dropping his bike and hurrying towards her. "Are you all right?"

"Ohhhhh!" she exclaimed, looking over her shoulder in alarm.

"It's me, Twitch," he said, reaching down to pick up her hat for her.

Quick as a shot, she grabbed it first and jammed it on her head.

"Are you hurt?" he asked, holding out his hand to help her up.

"No, no." Her voice wobbled as if she were about to cry. "I think I'm in shock."

Twitch guided her to a bench and sat her down.

"There was a fox!" she told him. "It was hurting the bird! I tried to make it stop."

"Bird?" Twitch turned and, in the undergrowth growing in the shadow of the trees that overhung the path, he spotted a bird he knew well. "Gilbert!"

The grey heron was cowering. Twitch saw that he had an injured wing. It hung down oddly at the bird's side. Gilbert was not a fearful bird. Normally he stalked along the canal like a king surveying his domain. He would stare out all who dared look at him and steal fish from fishermen's nets. Twitch peered up into the trees above the heron and spotted a mess of sticks in the nook of a branch. Had Gilbert built a nest?

"Oh, it was horrid." Mrs Drake's eyes were wide as she clutched Twitch's arm. "A fox had that poor bird in its mouth. I didn't know what to do! I hit the fox with my walking stick." She held up her beautifully carved wooden stick with a silver duck's head for a handle. "The fox dropped the bird, then went for me. I jumped back, slipped and fell. The fox ran away." She looked over at Gilbert. "Do you think the bird is all right? Look at his wing! Poor thing! What can we do?"

"Do you have a phone?" Twitch asked.

"Yes."

"There's a vet near the Aves Wood car park. Call them and tell them what's happened. They'll come out and look at him."

"It's very early," Mrs Drake said.

"They have an emergency twenty-four-hour service. I've called it a few times."

"I was out for a morning walk," she told him as she took her phone from her handbag. "Merle's so nervous about the competition, I thought it best to leave him to it. He's back at the campsite sorting through his fishing gear. He fished all day yesterday and barely caught a thing." Mrs Drake looked at Twitch's face and paused. "I'm sorry. I've forgotten your name."

"Corvus Featherstone, but everyone calls me Twitch."

"Ah, yes, you're the ornithologist. Forgive me. That fox gave me such a shock. My thoughts are scattered like seeds on the wind." She looked down at her phone. "Do you know the number? Oh no, hold on a second, I've got it. It's here on the Internet." She typed in the number of the vet. "You must spend all your time in these woods?"

"I've come here since I was little," Twitch replied, looking up. He wondered if Gilbert had found a mate. He knew that herons shared incubation duties and that foxes were rather partial to a heron's egg. Gilbert must have been protecting his nest.

"I'll bet you're a Scout; coming to my aid like that, you must be." Evelyn Drake pressed the button to make the call and Twitch saw she had a nasty scratch on her wrist from her struggle with the fox.

"No. My friends and I have a birding group called the Twitchers," he told her. "We've got a hide down by the pond."

"How wonderful!" Mrs Drake put the phone to her ear, looked over at Gilbert and her eyes filled with tears. "Poor chap. I do hope he's going to be OK." Her call was answered, and she launched into an explanation about the hurt bird. "Type of bird?" She looked at Twitch in a panic.

"Grey heron."

"Yes. It's a grey heron," Mrs Drake repeated. "I'm by Aves Lock. Great, see you shortly. Bye now." She put the phone back into her bag. "I think I'll sit here until the vet arrives," she told him. "But there's no point in both of us hanging around. Don't you worry, I'll make sure Gilbert is all right. I'm grateful to you for stopping. You've been a real help, Twitch." She beamed at him. "Thank you."

"Thank you for saving Gilbert from the fox," Twitch said, getting back on his bike. "I hope Mr Drake does well in the competition today."

"Oh, he won't," Mrs Drake said with a chuckle. "But don't tell him I said that!" And she waved as Twitch pedalled away.

Once he'd reached the still waters of the pond, it didn't take Twitch long to spot the two white wading birds. They were having breakfast, stalking through the shallow waters of the east bank, heads dipped, moving from side to side through the water until they detected a tiny fish or insect, when their beaks would snap shut. Retracing his steps, Twitch headed for the boggy east shore, hidden behind a forest of bulrushes. He left the footpath, taking a narrow animal track, dropping into a crouch as he scurried along the almost invisible winding way through the bed of tall reeds. As he approached the edge of the pond he slowed, moving with a calm grace, disturbing as few plants as possible.

Pushing his breath out over his teeth and moving his lips, he made a whispering whistle sound, *"pssswwwizz pssswwwizz!"* It flushed birds from their nests and, as they rose into the sky, he was alerted and knew where not to tread. Taking a slow and systematic approach to searching for the spoonbill nest, he scanned each area before moving onto the next. His eyes fixed on a tangle of sticks several metres up a willow tree that leaned over the water. Becoming excited, he crept closer, but soon saw it was an old nest and falling to pieces. It reminded him of Gilbert's nest, and guessed it had once belonged to a heron.

Huffing out a sigh of frustration, he took a couple of photographs of it, then looked across the water. The birds were no longer visible. Perhaps they weren't nesting on the east bank after all. He hadn't seen a nest on the west shoreline, nor was there one on the north side, where the hide was.

He turned to the south. Beyond the water was a jungle of briars, ferns and nettles. It was a thin stretch of land between the pond and the River Bridd. In summer, it was impassable. The path was overgrown and the ground was often flooded. If the spoonbills are nesting on the south side, Twitch thought, at least they'll be safe.

He climbed up into the willow tree to get a better look. Using his camera lens as a telescope, he surveyed the south bank, soon spotting a flash of white through the reeds. He smiled. Yes. It was one of the spoonbills. Was it the female building her nest?

Waiting patiently, staring through his camera, Twitch was rewarded with the sight of the male spoonbill arriving with a beak full of twigs. Snapping a picture of the domestic scene, he felt a thrill of joy. The wading birds had picked a good, secure spot to build their nest. If the Twitchers could just catch the thief before they started laying, everything might be all right.

15

LURES AND BAIT

Jack steeled himself before leaping directly into the path of the approaching figure. "Halt! Who goes there?" he cried at the silhouette beyond the thicket of ferns.

A familiar face appeared through the leaves. "It's me!" Twitch said, with a smile.

"Oh!" exhaled Terry from behind Jack. "Thank goodness!"

Jack turned and stared at Terry, who was clutching the microphone dish, wearing his headphones, and looking relieved. He shook his head. "You need to be a bit braver."

"I like the detecting part, not the catching," Terry replied. "Call it survival instinct."

"We heard someone sneaking about, running through the undergrowth and generally being suspicious," Jack told Twitch. "We came to check it out."

"Jack thought you might be the egg thief," Terry said. "He was ready to march you down to the police station."

Jack shrugged. "You could've been the thief."

"Sorry to disappoint you," Twitch said. "But, it's good your microphone picked up my sneaking about. I was trying to be quiet."

"What are you doing over this side of the wood?" Jack asked as they made their way back to the hide.

"I'll tell you when we're with the others."

The rest of the Twitchers were sitting on their logs in the cabin. Tara was handing out sweets. "There you are!" she said warmly, offering the Tupperware. "These are baklava. Ozuru came over last night and we did some baking. They are filo pastry with almonds, sugar syrup, rose water and pistachios. Want one?"

"They smell great." Jack hadn't had breakfast and was hungry after a night keeping watch with Terry. He chose the largest in the box and took a big bite.

"You didn't sleep in my tracksuit, did you?" Ava asked Terry, eyeing him up and down.

"No," Terry replied, his mouth full of baklava.

"Who's ready to report?" Jack asked.

"I'll go first," Ozuru said, opening his notebook. "I went to the police station and reported the missing bullfinch eggs to Constable Greenwood. He was on duty."

"What did he say?" Twitch asked.

"That he couldn't record the missing bullfinch eggs as a theft because we don't have any proof that someone took them. He was nice, but I don't think he was taking me seriously.

"They would've taken you seriously if you were a grown-up." Ava scowled.

"He's not leading the falcon egg case. It's someone called Inspector Khan."

Jack wrote this down in his notebook.

"That must be the woman I saw talking to him up the pike on Friday," Twitch said.

"She's working with the NWCU," Ozuru said. "Constable Greenwood said they don't have enough officers to set up patrols to stop people from stealing eggs. They're relying on the public stepping in if they see it happening. That's why they put up the posters."

"Was he helpful at all?" Jack asked.

"He did give me some information." Ozuru flicked over the page of his notebook. "The new land manager of Mord Hall called the police at six a.m. on Friday morning to report the falcon eggs stolen…"

"Mord Hall has a new land manager?" Twitch butted in.

"Yes. Constable Greenwood says the grouse hunting has stopped. The moor is going to be rewilded. A woman called" – Ozuru looked down at the page – "Ms Seeton is the land manager. She's moved into the old gamekeeper's cottage."

"I wouldn't want to live there." Tara shuddered.

"Ms Seeton noticed the falcons were distressed and making a racket. She went up the pike and saw the eggs were gone. She called the police at six a.m. but they couldn't get any officers up to investigate until late afternoon. Constable Greenwood explained that their priority is people who need help, and there wasn't much they could do for the birds once the eggs were gone."

Twitch tutted and shook his head.

"Go on," Jack prompted Ozuru. "This is good intel."

"He didn't want to say at first, but eventually Constable Greenwood told me that the people they know were up the pike on Thursday, early evening, were Twitch, Mr Bettany with his granddaughter Pippa, Mrs Dollopman walking her pack of dogs, an unidentified young man, tall, thin, with a rucksack on his back…"

"Henley Brandy," Jack said, nodding.

"…and a middle-aged lady in a burgundy hat, slacks and boots, with a walking stick."

Jack looked at Twitch. "Evelyn Drake! She's on our suspect list."

"I don't think she's our thief," Twitch said. "I saw her this morning. A fox attacked Gilbert, the grey heron, right in front of her. It was after his nest. She rescued Gilbert by whacking the fox with her stick. The fox went for her, scratched her hand and she fell. She was really upset. Poor Gilbert has a damaged wing. Evelyn Drake saved him. Someone like that doesn't steal birds' eggs." He shook his head. "Plus, she had no idea what kind of bird Gilbert was. She doesn't know enough to be an egg thief."

"I still think we should investigate her," Jack said. "A good detective considers everyone a suspect until proven otherwise."

"I'm telling you. It's Jed Butler," Twitch said.

"It could be someone that no one saw," Terry pointed out.

"Actually, we have an update on Jed Butler," Ava announced, "don't we, girls?" Tara and Tippi nodded. "Or should I say ... Martin Shrike!"

Jack could tell from their pleased looks that they'd discovered something important, and he leaned forward as Tara pulled out a piece of paper with an article printed on it. He glimpsed the headline *Notorious Egg Thief Caught!*

"This article is from six years ago," Tara said. "Ava had the idea that we should do an Internet search on the name of everyone in the Canal Masters to see what came up."

"Nothing did come up, or nothing interesting anyway," Ava told them. "That guy we met yesterday, Phil Gordon – he's won the Canal Masters three times. He's a pro. Anyway, Tippi suggested we should search for stories about egg thieves and we found this." She pushed the page into the middle of the table so they could all see. "His name isn't Jed Butler. It's Martin Shrike. But look at the picture. It's him!"

"I knew it!" Twitch exclaimed as Jack hurriedly read the article.

"It says he used to steal eggs to order!" Jack told them. "That people paid him five thousand pounds for a peregrine falcon egg!"

"The nest he robbed on the pike was worth twenty-five thousand pounds!" Terry whistled.

"Actually, twenty thousand because—" Jack stopped speaking as he felt a sharp pain under the table and saw the glare Ava was giving him.

"I didn't know wild bird eggs could be worth such big money!" Twitch looked horrified.

"How would you?" Tara said. "You're not a criminal."

"We need to take this to the police station imme-diately," Twitch said. "It must have been Jed Butler, or Martin Shrike, who stole those eggs."

"But we still don't have any proof," Jack said.

"What about the climbing gear in his car?" Terry asked.

"That's not proof," Jack said. "He could genuinely be into climbing. We need to find the eggs for the police to arrest him, or a witness to the theft, or preferably both." There was a silence as they thought about what to do.

"We need to keep a watch on Jed Butler," Twitch said.

"Agreed." Jack nodded. "If we catch him in the act, or with some stolen eggs, the police will be able to arrest him. But I still want us to keep investigating our other suspects, just in case."

"It's competition day," Ozuru said. "Jed will be by the canal all day."

"We should get down there." Twitch was on his feet.

"Wait, Twitch, I want to record a full report of your encounter with Evelyn Drake. If she was on the pike on Thursday, she's a suspect."

"Sure," Twitch said, heading for the door. "I'll tell you on the way. You can record it on your phone."

"They are doing the draw for pegs at nine o'clock, at Aves Lock," Ozuru said, hurrying to catch up with him.

Ava looked at her watch. "That's in twenty minutes."

"What are we waiting for?" Tippi said. "Let's go."

Jack suddenly found himself alone in the hide. He pinned the printed article to the case map and gathered up his notebook and pen. He resisted the urge to rush after the others. The evidence against Jed Butler was building, but he didn't want to assume. He had questions about Henley Brandy and Evelyn Drake. And what about the names Ozuru had discovered from Constable Greenwood: Mrs Dollopman, Mr Bettany and Pippa. He had reasons to suspect Pippa too. No, he must keep an open mind.

When Jack finally caught up with the others, Terry was swinging his head from left to right, scanning the area. "What are you doing?"

"I'm on the lookout for Pam," Terry replied. "I'm not falling for another one of her stupid tricks."

Twitch was talking to Ozuru. "If I want to get Jed Butler talking about fishing, what kind of questions should I ask?"

"You could ask him what his biggest catch is. Or what sort of lures or bait he's using..."

"Lures or bait? What's that?" Tara asked.

"A lure is fake fish food," Ozuru explained, "like a plastic worm, a small metal fish, or a fly made from feathers. You have to keep casting your line to make them look alive and real. Bait *is* real fish food, like maggots."

"Maggots!" Tippi pulled a face and stuck out her tongue. "Ewww."

"What does your dad use?" Jack asked.

"Depends on where he's fishing, but he'll use bread, maggots or a lure."

"Where does he get his maggots from?" Tippi asked.

"He buys them from the fishing shop."

"People sell maggots?" Tippi was astonished to learn this.

"There are people gathered at Aves Lock." Terry pointed. "I spy Jed Butler."

"Or should we call him Martin Shrike?" Ava waggled her eyebrows.

On the other side of the canal, beside the lock, about thirty people were milling around on a patch of grass furnished with two picnic tables. Beyond it was the car park for the private fishing lake.

"Dad!" Ozuru called out, crossing the lock gates and going to his father's side.

There came a murmur from the crowd of competitors as they parted to let a ruddy-faced man in a wax jacket through.

"I think the draw is about to start," Ava said.

Jack pulled out his notebook and pen, watching as two plastic bowls were ceremonially placed on one of the picnic tables. The man in the wax jacket pulled out a folded piece of paper from each bowl.

"Peg seven. Henley Brandy," he called out, putting the papers aside and taking out another two. "Peg three. Beryl Crocker."

A round woman wearing a long beige raincoat and a bucket hat shuffled forward.

"Peg one. Vernon Boon." There was a pause. Everyone looked around.

"Did he say Vernon Boon?" Jack asked Twitch, and was surprised to see their classmate come running out of the car park, followed by his dad clutching a cool box and a fishing rod. "I didn't know Vernon liked fishing."

"Is he still an honorary Twitcher?" Ava asked.

"He lost interest in us after he joined the Junior Police Cadets," Terry replied. "Like Pam and Clem, Vernon is only interested in us if we're solving crimes."

"I'm here!" Vernon bellowed and they repeated his peg number.

Jack was a bit in awe of Vernon. Despite being the same age, Vernon's voice had already broken and he could even grow facial hair.

"Peg nine. Dr Sawa."

"Nine must be a good peg," Tara said. "Dr Sawa is smiling."

"Peg two. Philip Gordon."

The competitive fisherman punched the air. Jack saw Jed Butler scowl and mutter something to Merle Drake, who nodded. Peg two must be a good spot on the canal. Jack took a second to study Evelyn Drake, who was standing beside her husband, ruddy-cheeked and smiling. He found himself agreeing with Twitch. She was an unlikely suspect.

"Peg five. Merle Drake."

Mr Drake shrugged, his lips narrowing into an accepting smile as Evelyn patted him on the arm.

"Peg six. Chris Merriman."

Chris raised his hand to show that he'd heard and grinned.

"What are you smiling for, Chris?" Phil Gordon guffawed. "That's a terrible spot, right below the lock gates."

"I'm here for the fishing, Phil," Chris replied, "not the winning."

Phil Gordon snorted.

"Peg ten. Kenneth Mulworthy."

"From Mord Hall!" Terry looked at Jack.

"Harry Bettany. Peg four." The man looked up. "We've had a message to say he'll be arriving late."

"Probably because of the shop," Twitch said.

"And finally, peg eight. Jed Butler."

Jack watched the scowling, shaven-headed man collect his fishing kit and stalk away. Jed Butler or Martin Shrike? They were one and the same. Jed knew about birds. He had talked to Phil Gordon about guillemot eggs, asked Twitch about eggs, had a previous record of egg theft and climbing gear in his car. He'd been in his car on Passerine Pike watching the police investigate the falcon egg theft. Jack had to admit, the case against the unlikable angler was undeniably strong.

16

SOMETHING FISHY

Jack clapped his hands together to get everyone's attention, then said in a low voice, "Twitch, Tara, you two watch Jed." Twitch nodded, pleased to have this assignment. "Ava, Tippi and I are going to take a trip up the canal to do a spot of investigating."

"I want to see if anyone knows about Martin Shrike," Ava muttered, her eyes looking left then right to check she wasn't overheard.

"No point in talking to Vernon," Terry said. "He won't know him. He's never entered a fishing competition before."

"Nor has Mr Bettany," Twitch added.

"But Vernon might have heard something about the egg thefts through the Junior Cadets," Tara said.

"I bet Beryl Crocker knows Jed, if she's won lots of competitions," Jack said.

"Uh-oh." Terry was looking across to where Ozuru and his dad were setting up on the other side of the canal. "Kenneth Mulworthy has peg ten, next to Dr Sawa! Do you think he's still cross with us about what happened at the Mord Hall Halloween Ball?"

"I guess you're about to find out," Jack said with a grin, thinking back to a night last autumn when he'd risked everything to save the life of a bearded vulture.

"Let's make like a banana and split," Ava said, and the group broke apart.

Merle Drake was sitting in his chair, two rods already propped on perches over the water. A knife lay on the ground at his feet. In his lap he had a pestle and mortar. He was grinding something in it. As the children approached, he paused and put on his cap.

Tippi marched right up to him and peered into his lap. "What are you doing?"

"Tippi!" Ava rushed over and Jack hurried after her.

"I'm making my secret bait recipe," Merle told Tippi. "The fish love it. You take a handful of chopped worms, a sprinkling of maggots and a spoonful of castors."

"What are castors?" Tippi peered at the tiny orange cylinders in the bowl.

"Fly pupae." Merle held up the pestle. "You crush them up to make them juicy."

"Ewww." Tippi pulled a face and he laughed.

"I crumble in a bit of bread to bind it all together." He reached into his mortar, gathered the wriggling mixture in his gloved hand, gave it a squeeze, and put it in a cup on the end of a plastic rod. "We pop it into the feeder pole, and" – he telescoped the rod out – "tip the bait into the water." He withdrew the rod. "Those lovely, crushed wrigglers will bring the fish."

Tippi stared open-mouthed at him.

"You sound like a pro! Do you enter a lot of fishing competitions, Mr Drake?" Ava asked, pulling Tippi away from him.

"I'm retired. Fishing competitions get me out and about. They give shape to the year."

"You must know some of the other competitors well," Jack said.

"The same names and faces pop up." He nodded. "Take young Henley, for instance. I've been in three or four competitions with him. The lad's beaten me every time. He's a fishing wizard."

"Do you know Jed Butler?" Jack asked. "I know Phil Gordon is the favourite to win, but I think Jed Butler is a dark horse."

"Really?" Merle's unruly eyebrows shot up. "I don't know the young man well. He keeps himself to himself.

Bit of a loner, you might say. Not very chatty. Not a bad fisherman, but not a particularly good one either. Spends half his time looking at birds."

Ava glanced at Jack. "Dr Sawa said the fisherman to look out for is Martin Shrike."

"Who?" Merle frowned. "Surely he means Phil Gordon. He's the man to beat today."

"Is your wife all right?" Jack asked. "Twitch said she was attacked by a fox this morning."

"Poor Evelyn." Merle nodded. "She stayed to see which peg I got and wish me luck, but she's gone back to the campsite now for a lie-down. You must thank your young friend for me." He took a chopping board from his tackle box and emptied a tub of worms onto it. Picking his knife up from the floor, he sliced them up. "This morning gave her quite a shock."

Seeing the look of horror on Tippi's face at the fate of the worms, Ava said, "Well, we'd better let you get on. Good luck."

"Who needs luck when you've got a special bait recipe," Merle said cheerily as they walked away.

As they strolled on, a flustered Mr Bettany ran past them, dumping a duffle bag down at his peg and yanking his fishing kit out.

"Morning," Jack greeted him as Mr Bettany speedily screwed his rod together.

"I need to get my hook in the water," Mr Bettany said, "catch up with the others."

"Have you met the other competitors?" Ava asked.

"Only the locals."

"What about him?" Tippi pointed down the canal to Jed Butler.

"Nope," Mr Bettany said, squinting down the canal. "Although, I did see him talking with Inspector Khan outside the shop the day before yesterday."

Jack's insides lurched. Were the police already on to Jed Butler? He knew it wasn't a race, and he was supposed to be helping the police, but secretly he wanted to be the first to unmask the egg thief.

"Come on, Tippi," Ava said, tugging at her sister. "Let's leave Mr Bettany to fish."

The newsagent smiled appreciatively as they walked on.

Beryl Crocker was standing at the canal's edge, peering into the water from the underbrim of her bucket hat. Her long brown coat was buttoned tightly over her big chest; her twig-like legs poked out the bottom. Jack could see that her ancient rod was already cast. A red float bobbed in the water. As they approached, she sat down and poured a cup of tea from her flask.

"Morning, Mrs Crocker," Jack said politely. "Dr Sawa says you're the one to beat today."

"That's kind." She smiled, taking a sip of the steaming tea. "But the fish will decide who the winner is."

"What's your secret?" Ava asked. "How did you get so good?"

"I study them." Beryl Crocker's mischievous green bead-like eyes looked up at them as she waved a hand at the water. "I don't fish blind, throwing out my line any old how. I watch and wait. I cast a line when I know there's a fish that wants to bite. Knowing a creature makes it easier to catch." She leaned towards them. "But I take great care to put the fish back when I'm done."

"Do you know Jed Butler?" Jack asked.

"Jed's a good lad." Beryl nodded. "I've beaten him in a few competitions. He could do with learning a bit more about the ways of fish!" Her cackle became a cough. She thumped her chest and took another sip of tea.

Jack was startled to hear affection for Jed, but he guessed she didn't know he was an egg thief.

"Have you ever competed against Martin Shrike?" Ava asked.

"Can't say that I have," Beryl replied after a moment's thought.

An awkward silence fell, and so Jack wished her luck and they moved on.

Phil Gordon had more fishing equipment than anyone else. Five rods of varying lengths and size were lying on the bank beside the champion fisherman. He was on his knees, peering into his tackle box, a large fibreglass shell with many internal compartments.

"We wanted to wish you luck," Ava said.

"Don't need it," Phil Gordon said, threading a fly onto a hook. "I know what I'm doing." He looked up. "I've got this one in the bag or, should I say, net!"

"I heard Martin Shrike was going to enter," Jack said, watching Phil's face intently.

"Who?" Phil said, tying the knot tight. Jack felt a little disappointed that no one had reacted to the name. Jed must have kept his past identity a secret. Twitch had told him eggers were secretive people.

"I don't think he's turned up." Ava looked at Jack enquiringly. There was only one more thing Jack wanted to test out.

"The kingfishers were out this morning," he said. "Did you see them?"

"Can't say that I did. Hope they haven't scared the fish."

Jack glanced at Ava and gave a faint shake of the head. Phil Gordon didn't show a flicker of interest in birds. The man was obsessed with fish.

"Let's go and say hello to Vernon," Jack said as they walked away. He pointed to the other side of the canal, where his classmate was sticking out his tongue, concentrating on tying off his line.

"I didn't know you like to fish," Jack called out, as they crossed the lock.

"Got a rod for Christmas," Vernon replied. "I'm having a go on my own, but Dad's coming back later to give me pointers."

"How's your Junior Police Cadets training going?" Ava asked.

"Brilliant." Vernon sniffed. "I'm definitely going to be a policeman when I grow up."

"We're investigating the egg thief," Tippi told him.

"The peregrine falcon eggs," Jack clarified.

"I heard about that," Vernon said. "Let me know if you need me to arrest anyone. I can do that now, you know."

"We have a prime suspect," Jack told him quietly. "He's taking part in the competition."

Vernon's head snapped up. "Who?"

"I found an article online, about a man called Martin Shrike," Ava said softly. "He went to jail for stealing eggs a few years ago. He's the fisherman with a shaved head on peg eight."

"Except, now he's calling himself Jed Butler," Jack added.

Vernon let out a low whistle. "Previous form!"

"Eggs only started going missing when he came to Briddvale," Tippi said.

"Want me to keep an eye on him for you?" Vernon asked eagerly.

Jack and Ava both nodded.

"We're closing in on him," Jack said. "We just need some evidence."

17

EASTER EGG

Jack considered what Mr Bettany had said, about seeing Jed Butler talking with a police officer, as they walked back on the opposite side of the canal to meet the others at Dr Sawa's peg. Surely, if the police had enough evidence to arrest him, they would have by now?

"Check it out," Ava said. "Dr Sawa looks like the cat that got the cream."

"Not bad, eh?" Dr Sawa gestured to his nets proudly. His first net was so full of squirming fish that he'd put out a second. "I had a bit of help," he admitted in a low voice. "From the man on peg seven."

"Henley Brandy?" Jack was surprised.

"He fired an enormous amount of bait into the water with his catapult," Ozuru explained. "Then a boat came along the canal and pulled his feed this way."

"Then," Terry said, "he put a speaker in the canal

and started playing sounds to the fish. They swam this way to get away from the noise. He's bonkers. He's got Meccano bolt-ons for his rod, like weird robot arms."

"Mr Butler benefitted too," Dr Sawa said, "but I do seem to have caught the lion's share of the fleeing fish." His eyes sparkled.

"Poor Henley Brandy!" Tara said.

"There's no way anyone is going to catch as many fish as you, Dad." Ozuru bounced on the balls of his toes. "You're going to win today's round and maybe the whole thing!"

"There's still Wednesday," Dr Sawa said cautiously. "I doubt I'll be lucky enough to draw a peg downstream from Mr Brandy twice. Somebody else may benefit next time. But" – his eyes sparkled – "it's looking good."

"Did you discover anything new about Jed Butler?" Twitch whispered.

"No one recognizes the name Martin Shrike," Jack replied. "And Beryl Crocker likes him! But get this, Mr Bettany saw Inspector Khan talking to Jed Butler outside the newsagent's on Saturday. The police must be on to him."

"They must know about his previous record," Twitch said. "The sooner they arrest him, the better."

"But they haven't arrested him yet," Jack pointed out. "There must be a reason."

"Perhaps they don't have enough evidence."

"I talked to Kenneth Mulworthy," Terry said. "He doesn't work at Mord Hall any more. He's the new manager of the Sozzled Stork pub. He didn't know anything about Jed Butler."

"Vernon is going to keep an eye on Jed for us today," Ava told Twitch. "So we can go back to the hide."

"Do you think we could get your boat?" Twitch asked Ozuru. "I'd like to get on the water." His voice fell to a whisper. "See if we can spot the spoonbill nest. We need to find out if there are any eggs in it yet."

"Terry and I can go and get the boat now," Ozuru said, looking at Terry. "You'll help me carry the dinghy to the hide, won't you?"

"Fine." Terry flicked back his hair and sighed. "Use me for my muscles."

Ava snorted.

Saying farewell to Dr Sawa, Ozuru and Terry scooted off to get the boat, while the other Twitchers returned to the hide.

"The nesting boxes are mostly empty," Ava said as they strolled through the trees.

"It's early in the season," Twitch told her. "New nests will be being built every day."

Jack was only half listening to the others talking, because he was thinking about Jed Butler. Why hadn't the police arrested him? They must know about his previous record. Was it a lack of evidence? Or was it something else?

"Jack." Twitch's voice shook him from his thoughts. "If we don't catch Jed Butler, he'll leave Briddvale and steal eggs somewhere else."

"Yeah," Jack agreed. "I know."

"He has to be stopped. This isn't just about the birds of Briddvale," Twitch said. "It's about birds everywhere."

"We're trying our best," Ava reassured him.

"We've taken an oath," Tara reminded him.

"I know." Twitch glanced about cautiously. "If the spoonbills have laid eggs, we're going to have to watch them twenty-four-seven."

"I've thought of something," Ava said. "Ozuru's boat. We don't want the thief to see it and use it."

"We'll make a cover for it," Tara said. "Camouflage it."

It was getting on for lunchtime when they reached the hide, so they grabbed their packed lunches and ate them sitting on the ground, looking out over the pond, listening to the babbling birds and the chirruping insects. Jack took out his notebook and wrote down everything he'd been told by the Canal Masters competitors that morning, hoping that something concrete would jump out at him. He pulled his phone from his pocket and got Twitch to recount his morning adventure with Evelyn Drake, Gilbert and the fox, and then he sat and thought about it.

"I still can't believe we've got spoonbills in Aves Wood," Tara said, watching them through her binoculars. She looked at her lenses, then at Twitch. "Do you want to borrow them?"

"It's OK," Twitch said, looking out over the water. "I can use my camera. It's funny, the thing I miss most is the weight of them, hanging around my neck. It made me feel calm and grounded. Without them I feel like a ship without an anchor."

Ava dusted sandwich crumbs from her hands and jumped up. "I'm going to get to work on the boat cover. Who wants to help?"

"Give me a sec," Jack said, stuffing his sandwich into his mouth.

The five of them circled the copse of hazel trees, cutting down slender, bendy branches. Using Twitch's Swiss Army knife, Ava and Jack gathered ferns, leafy twigs and blackberry runners, while Tara, Tippi and

Twitch sat on the ground weaving the hazel branches into a giant rectangular frame, through which they threaded the ferns, twigs and runners. By the time Ozuru and Terry arrived carrying the dinghy upside down on their heads, one fore, one aft, the cover was almost finished.

"Is that to put over the boat? It's ace!" Ozuru said as they put the boat down beside the water.

"What is going on with my phone?" Terry yanked his ancient, cracked smartphone from his pocket. "All morning it's been vibrating like I'm getting millions of messages, but I can't see them! The bottom of the screen has been black since I fell in the canal." He tapped at the screen then shook the phone violently and glared at it, pressing the button. Then he frowned and made a strangled sound.

"What's the matter?" Ozuru asked.

"I *am* getting millions of messages!" Terry was going purple. "Pam's video of me is online!" He looked around. "Who's got a decent phone? I need to see it right now!"

Jack pulled his phone from his pocket. "There's no signal here. You'll have to take it to Crowther Bridge to watch it."

Terry grabbed Jack's phone and sprinted away. Jack glanced at the others. They all wanted to see that video.

After a second, they ran after him. When they arrived at the bridge, Terry had found the video. He pressed play.

Pamela introduced Clem in his green ivy-clad body stocking, explaining what they planned to do. The first minute was a montage of people walking past him, being annoyed when he jumped out then walking on. It cut to the Twitchers coming along the towpath.

"That's me!" Tippi said.

As Jack watched, Tippi let out her blood-curdling scream and Terry fell backwards. He glimpsed a flash of silver on the other side of the canal, in the branches of a tree. The video scrubbed backwards, playing the scream and fall again, then again. It cut to a close-up of Terry thrashing about in the water and Jack saw the top of a familiar elfin face peeping over the lock gates.

Pam had added a piece of comedy trombone music, which played as Terry stood up, duckweed hanging from his dark curls. She appeared on the screen. "Wham! Bam! You've been pranked by Pam!"

"Look at the views!" Terry groaned. "Nearly a hundred thousand!" He handed the phone back to Jack. "This is a nightmare. I'll never live it down. My brothers will tease me for ever."

"They might not have seen it," Ava said.

"Who do you think was messaging me about

it?" Terry looked miserable. "I'll never be able to get a girlfriend now. I'm going to die alone."

"Ignore it," Twitch said, patting his friend on the shoulder. "We've got a case to solve and birds to protect. When we catch the thief, people will have something else to talk about. They'll forget all about the video."

"It's on the Internet!" Terry exclaimed. "It'll still be there when I'm an old man."

"You should play a prank on her," Tippi said, leaning her head against Terry's side in sympathy. "See how she likes it."

"That is not a bad idea!" Terry straightened up. "Revenge!"

"I don't think we should be too angry with Pam," Jack said, studying the phone screen. "She's done us a favour. She's captured a clue! Look!"

18

BRANDY SNAPS

Twitch was unsure what to make of seeing Pippa Bettany's face in the background of Pam's video. Jack had zoomed in and it was clear as day that she had been peering over Aves Lock, watching them.

"I'm moving Pippa Bettany up the suspect list," Jack announced as they returned to the hide.

"But we agreed, Pippa is too young to be a serious suspect." Twitch felt a spark of annoyance. It was obvious to everyone, including the police, that Jed Butler was the thief. Investigating Pippa was a waste of time. He wished Jack didn't take his detecting so seriously sometimes.

"Pippa and Mr Bettany were some of the last people to see the falcons' nest with the eggs still in it on Thursday evening," Jack reminded him.

"Why is that girl following us?" Tippi asked, looking excited.

"She's spying," Jack said. "She might be worried that we're on to her."

"Thieves do sneak about." Tippi nodded.

"That doesn't prove anything." Twitch pointed at the screenshot Jack had on his phone. "Pippa loves birds. She knows a lot about them. She probably just wants to be a Twitcher."

"You said the egg thief would know about birds," Jack retorted. "And that they would be obsessive."

"You must admit, her behaviour is pretty obsessive," Terry said.

Twitch fell silent. Pippa was annoying, but he didn't believe she was an egg thief. Egg thieves were fanatical in a dark way, not in an enthusiastic, excited way. They were ruthless, which was not a word he would use to describe Pippa. And, though he found her misplaced hero-worship embarrassing, Twitch had listened to enough of Pippa's monologues about birds to be sure she'd never harm one.

"You are right about Pippa being young," Jack said. "But it's possible she could be working with an accomplice." He paused. "What about her grandad?"

"You suspect Mr Bettany now?" Twitch stopped in his tracks.

"Is it possible he and Pippa are in on it together?" Jack asked.

"I told you, it's not someone local." Twitch shook his head. "If someone from Briddvale collected eggs, they'd disappear every year in nesting season."

"Or," Jack countered, "they've only just got old enough to start the hobby of egg collecting and this is the first spring they've had the chance."

"Jed Butler has the climbing gear," Twitch replied. "We should be concentrating on him."

"I agree he is a strong suspect," Jack said. "But if the police know about his criminal record, why haven't they arrested him?"

"Maybe they don't know about the climbing gear," Ava suggested.

"The thief is Jed Butler," Twitch insisted, feeling himself becoming angry. "I know it."

"I'm just saying we shouldn't rule anyone out." Jack bristled.

"So, what do we do now?" Terry said, stepping between the two of them.

"Check the spoonbill nest," Twitch said, walking on. "We need to know if they are in immediate danger."

"Great," Terry said, herding everyone forward. "Let's get that boat on the water, take a look in the nest, then swing back to find out if Dr Sawa has won today's fishing trial."

"Me, Tara and Tippi are going to stay in the hide tonight," Ava told Twitch. "We brought our camping stuff this morning."

"But we have to go home and have dinner first," Tara added.

When they reached the pond, Jack helped Twitch lift the boat into the water. Climbing in first, Twitch took his camera from Ava. Then Jack clambered on board and sat next to him. Ava got into the prow, sitting on the floor.

"Paddle until we're in the middle of the pond," Twitch said to Jack. "We'll lift out the oars and float, so the birds get used to us being there. Then, slowly, we'll move to the spot where I saw the male spoonbill gathering nesting materials this morning. I want to be certain it definitely is on the south bank."

"If we can find the exact location of the nest," Ava said, "we might be able to think of ways to protect it."

Twitch dipped his oar in the water and pulled back. Jack matched each of his strokes and, as they rowed in unison, he found his irritation with Jack subsiding. Ava had her binoculars to her eyes and was scanning the far shore. In the middle of the pond, they lifted their oars out of the water, setting them down in the bottom of the boat. Their dinghy gently bobbed and turned in the water as they searched for the birds.

Twitch glimpsed a flash of white, focused his camera lens and took a picture.

"Spoonbill?" Jack asked, every muscle of his face keen and alert.

Twitch shook his head, pointing and whispering, "Ringed plover in the reeds over there."

Jack trained his binoculars, becoming very still as he watched the small wading bird. Twitch realized with sudden affection that it was a new bird for Jack's list.

They'd been floating about in the middle of the pond for about a quarter of an hour when Ava let out a high gasp. The male spoonbill stalked out of the reeds on the south side of the pond. "There!" she whispered.

The three of them watched the bird in silence, then Twitch picked up his oar and Jack followed. Dipping them in the water, they made one stroke together, lifting the oars and letting the boat glide gently towards the south shore. Twitch controlled the direction of the dinghy with the tip of his oar. Two more such strokes and they were metres from the reed bed. Bulrushes stood before them, poker straight, like a sentry barring entry.

Jack grabbed Twitch's arm and suddenly he saw it too. A nest on the tangled bank of the south shore, barely a metre from the water. Sitting on it, very still, was the female spoonbill.

Twitch switched places with Ava, so he was crouched at the front of the boat. Raising his camera, he focused his lens and took a series of pictures of the nesting bird. She was laying eggs. He was almost certain of it. Then he photographed the water's edge, the land, the trees and the plants growing around the nest, in the hope that it would help them come up with a way to protect it. When he was done, he signalled to Jack and Ava, who slipped the oars into the water and rowed back to the hide.

At five o'clock, the Twitchers arrived at Aves Lock in time to hear a bell ring. All anglers were instructed to withdraw their rods from the water. The judges visited each peg, weighing the competitor's catches. Twitch watched with interest as the judges recorded the weight of each catch onto a clipboard, before releasing the fish back into the canal.

Phil Gordon was uncharacteristically quiet, frowning as he watched the weighing.

A goggle-eyed Henley Brandy started huffing like a steam engine when he saw the volume of Dr Sawa's catch. "They're my fish!" he protested, crossing his arms.

"Is there a problem, Mr Brandy?" asked one of the judges, a portly man with a moustache like a sweeping brush.

"Dr Sawa's net is full of my fish!" Henley said.

"Are you accusing Dr Sawa of stealing your fish, Mr Brandy?"

"No." Henley stuck his chin out. "Well. Yes. Thing is, a boat dragged my bait down to his peg … and … and…"

"It's the Canal Masters, Mr Brandy. There are boats on canals. That's the challenge of the competition."

"But … there were no fish for me to catch!" Henley was becoming agitated, and Twitch noticed that the knuckles on both of his hands were raw and scratched. He felt a flicker of uncertainty. Was he being too blinkered in his assumption that Jed was the egger? But no, he felt it in his bones. The shaven-headed man was the thief.

"The competition's not over yet," the judge said. "Perhaps you'll draw a better peg on Wednesday."

"You've done better than me," Mr Bettany said. "I only caught one fish today."

"Me too," Vernon Boon said, proudly. "It was a decent size." He held up his hands to demonstrate the length of his fish.

Jed Butler pointed to his net. The man had a hard, unreadable expression as the judges weighed his catch. He'd caught some fish, but not enough to challenge the larger catches. He didn't seem too bothered about it. It was impossible to know whether he was happy with his day's fishing or not. Twitch glanced about. It suddenly occurred to him that the police might be watching, but he saw no officers. He wondered if Jed used the cover of fishing competitions to travel about the country so he could steal different types of birds' eggs.

Once all the weighing was done, Dr Sawa was announced the winner of the day. Beryl Crocker came second. Phil Gordon came third.

Henley Brandy stalked back to his peg and kicked over his camping chair. "I'll beat you all on Wednesday," he shouted angrily. "You see if I don't!"

19

HENS' TEETH

Twitch gave himself the job of planning the protection of the spoonbill nest, and eventually persuaded Jack that one of them should go to the police station and tell Constable Greenwood that they suspected Jed Butler was the egg thief. Twitch felt certain that, after the two cases he'd helped Constable Greenwood with last year, the police officer would act on their suspicions. Terry and Ozuru volunteered to do it on their way home. The girls went home for dinner, excited about returning for the night watch. Jack was following Jed back to the campsite to make sure he didn't steal any eggs. Jack said he would also watch Henley and the Drakes as he wasn't one hundred per cent certain Jed was their thief.

As he pedalled home, Twitch considered the kind of traps or signals he might build around the nesting waders to protect them. He wondered if anyone else knew there were spoonbills in Aves Wood. It was too much to hope that they'd been the only people to have spotted them, although the Canal Masters had kept everyone busy and out of the woods these past few days. As he approached his house, Twitch was surprised to see Pippa Bettany sitting on his doorstep. She had a red tin on her lap and her face was pale and serious.

"Hello," Twitch greeted her. "What are you doing here?"

"I need to talk to you." She stood up, clutching the square tin to her chest.

"I'm a bit busy—"

"It's urgent," she cut him off.

"OK…" Twitch was taken aback by her forcefulness. "You'd better come in." Stepping past her, he noticed her looking about fearfully. "Are you all right?" He opened the door. "You're not in trouble, are you?" Jack's accusations flashed into his mind.

"I need your help," Pippa said, following him into the house.

"Sit down," Twitch said, pointing at the kitchen table. "Do you want a glass of squash?" He took out two glasses without waiting for her reply. "I'm thirsty." He made her a drink and put it on the table. "What is it that you need my help with?"

"This." Pippa placed the scratched red tin down. There was an old-fashioned advert for gravy on the lid. She prised it off with her small fingers. Twitch gasped when he saw what was inside.

Nestled in cotton wool were birds' eggs. He counted twenty, all from different birds.

"Where did you get these?" His voice was a whisper. "You didn't ... collect them?"

"No!" Pippa exclaimed.

Twitch noticed she was fidgeting nervously with the edge of her long-sleeved T-shirt, twisting and pulling at it. Was she lying? Had Jack been right?

"Whose are they?"

"Um." She turned her head away. "I can't tell you."

Looking down at the eggs, Twitch saw the mottled fawn egg of the barn swallow, and his skin prickled as his eyes lit upon the faded pale blue and spotted egg of the bullfinch. He recognized a tiny greenish-white egg marked and spotted with brown as belonging to the house sparrow, and the beautiful blue-green lightly speckled blackbird's egg. Then his body went rigid. There was a larger egg. It was the size of a small hen's egg, cream in colour but almost entirely eclipsed by irregular rust-brown markings. "That's a peregrine falcon egg!"

"Is it?" Pippa squeaked.

"Are these yours, Pippa?"

"No!" She shook her head vehemently. "I promise. They aren't."

"Where did you get them? You must tell me."

"I... I..." Her eyes darted around as if she were searching for an answer. "I found them!"

"Where?" Twitch studied her face.

"I... I can't say," she replied, slumping miserably into a chair at the table.

"You know it's illegal to collect birds' eggs?"

"They're not mine!" she protested.

"It's a crime to even possess them."

"It is?" She looked up at him with big, frightened eyes.

"Why did you bring these to me?"

"Because I didn't know what to do. When I found them... I... I..." Her bottom lip began to tremble, and her eyes filled with tears. "I thought people might think they belonged to the egg thief ... but ... but..." She made a hiccupping noise as if she were about to burst into tears. "I don't want to go to prison!"

"Do you know who collected these eggs?" Twitch asked softly.

Pippa's head drooped so he couldn't see her eyes. "No," she whispered, and Twitch suspected she was lying. He wanted to push her to tell him the truth, but he could see the tiniest thing would cause her to collapse and cry. "But it wasn't you?"

Pippa shook her head emphatically.

"You can tell me where you found them," he coaxed gently. "I won't tell anyone."

Pippa shook her head resolutely. "I can't."

Twitch stared at the tin. It made him feel funny, as if it were a ticking time bomb. "I think you should take it to the police."

"NO!" Pippa looked panicked. She pleaded with him. "Can't you take it? Say you found it in the bushes or something… I… I…" Tears spilled from her eyes and her bottom lip trembled. "I'm scared."

"OK, OK, don't go getting upset." Twitch wondered what he should do. If he took the tin to the hide, the others would think it was concrete evidence that Pippa was the thief, but he didn't believe that. He was certain it was Jed Butler. And then he realized they'd interviewed everyone about the theft, except for Pippa. "You and your grandad visited the peregrine falcon nest on Thursday evening, before it was robbed." Her expression became mournful, and she nodded. "I don't suppose you saw anyone up there, on Passerine Pike?"

"I saw Ms Seeton in her Land Rover on the Mord

Estate, and a lady walking fast, talking on her phone, with lots of dogs on leads. And when we were walking up the hill, a man was coming down, on his own, but I didn't know him."

"What did he look like?"

"Um, just a man, wearing a blue coat. At least, I think it was blue. It could've been black, or grey." She smiled apologetically. "I didn't really pay him much attention."

"Did he have a shaved head?"

"No. He had hair." Tippi screwed her face up as she tried to remember. "It was grey."

"How old was he?"

"Really old. Like forty or fifty, maybe sixty. But he didn't have glasses or a beard."

Twitch took out his notebook and wrote this down. He had no idea who Pippa was describing. It wasn't Henley. The list Ozuru had got from Constable Greenwood hadn't mentioned this man. This was someone new.

"What are you going to do with the eggs?" Pippa asked, looking at the tin as if it might try to bite her.

"Take them to the police station."

"You mustn't tell anyone I gave them to you!" she pleaded.

"It's all right," Twitch soothed her. "I'll say I found them buried in the woods." He felt a pinch of anxiety at the thought of telling a lie to the police, but he didn't want the eggs in his house. He could see dust in the old tin. They didn't look freshly collected. He didn't think they could be the eggs that had gone missing in the past week. They were someone's old collection and he suspected he knew who they belonged to.

"Oh, thank you, Twitch." Pippa flung her arms around him. "You're the best, you really are. I knew coming to you was the right thing to do."

"It's getting late," Twitch said. "You should go home before someone starts worrying about you."

"I will." Pippa hurried to the front door. "Thank you."

Closing the door, Twitch looked back down the hall at the tin on the table. Jack would want him to photograph it for evidence. In the morning, he'd take it to the police station and hand it in. He didn't think he could get into trouble for finding a tin of eggs in the woods. They weren't his after all.

Sitting down in front of the tin, Twitch carefully lifted out each delicate chalky eggshell from the cotton wool, examined it, then returned it. He could see the horrible hole where each egg had been emptied.

Noticing a white egg tinged with pink and decorated with black flecks, he frowned. It was about three centimetres in length and didn't immediately register in Twitch's encyclopedic bird brain. He'd never seen an egg like it. Fetching his books from the living room, it took him a little while to work out that it was a golden oriole egg. He had never seen the shy golden yellow and black bird. Populations had been in decline for years and barely bred here any longer. The egg he was holding was as rare as hens' teeth. This egg collection had to be twenty years old. It confirmed his suspicion that these couldn't be the eggs that had been going missing from Aves Wood and Passerine Pike.

He put the lid on the box, but as soon as the eggs were hidden, he felt an urge to look at them again. They were such perfectly beautiful things. Tiny bedchambers for baby birds.

I'll just take one more look, Twitch thought, lifting the lid again, and then I'll put them away.

20

THE EGG ARTIST

Twitch picked up the peregrine falcons' egg and tried to get into the mindset of an egger. "Think!" he told himself. But all that came into his mind was the loss of the fragile life that should have hatched out of the chalky shell. Tears welled up in his eyes. He blinked them back angrily. This was no good. Crying wasn't going to help him protect the spoonbills or catch Jed Butler.

"Why can't he collect something else?" he muttered, putting the egg back in the tin. "Like teapots or stamps." He paused. Eggs were commonplace and at the same time a kind of magic, a symbol of life. If you collected stamps, you bought them. But to collect eggs you had to steal and kill. With this thought, he glimpsed the mind of the thief. The kind of person who would steal a life, thousands of lives, who would enjoy the thrill of an illegal act, risk their own life doing it, who would covet their secret forbidden treasure as a goblin covets gold, and he shivered. Jed Butler was a very dangerous man.

An idea pecked at Twitch's brain. Pushing his chair back, he went to the kitchen dresser and took out his mother's battered old address book. He found the page he was looking for and ran his finger down the column of names. Yes! He was here! Twitch took out his phone and dialled the number.

"Hello, is that Mr Landrow? Hi. Um, you won't remember me. My name is Twitch... I mean, Corvus Featherstone. I'm Tom Featherstone's grandson." There was silence. "We met seven years ago at my grandad's funeral. I was six..."

"Goodness! Yes. I remember. I'm sorry for your loss, Corvus. Your grandfather was a good friend."

"Thank you. I miss him every day..." Twitch swallowed, suddenly finding himself confronting the abyss of grief in his chest that his binoculars used to bridge. How could he have been so careless to have lost them? "Um..." He thought of the spoonbills and pushed on. "I don't know if you remember, but at the funeral, you gave me a guillemot's egg made from resin..."

"I remember."

"I still have it. It's on our mantelpiece. It looks so real."

"I try and make them as close to the real thing as possible."

"Do you still make eggs?" Twitch's heartbeat quickened as he came to the reason for his call.

"Of course." Mr Landrow chuckled. "It's my job. You'd be surprised how many people around the world want lifelike birds' eggs for filming TV shows, or to study in universities, or display in their homes."

"Oh, good." Twitch felt a glimmer of hope. "Have you ever made spoonbill eggs?"

"Do you know, I haven't. There's not much call for them. Spoonbills rarely nest in this country."

"I know, but … do you think you could make spoonbill eggs?"

"I'm certain of it," Mr Landrow replied. "Why?"

Twitch told Mr Landrow about the nesting pair of spoonbills in Aves Wood and about the egg thief. He explained that he was trying to find a way to protect the birds' eggs and had thought of a plan, but that it depended on Mr Landrow. The egg artist listened attentively to him and, when Twitch had finished, he grunted.

"I'd be glad to help you, Corvus," the kind man said. "Now, listen, it usually takes me a day to make the eggs and a day to paint them, but I've not made spoonbill eggs before, so I'm going to have to study them and make a new mould. That all takes time."

"But, sir." Twitch's voice was urgent. "The spoonbills were laying today. We're patrolling the wood as best we can, but it's impossible to be everywhere and the egg thief comes out at night. We don't have time."

"I see. Well then, I'll make you a clutch of spoonbill eggs as fast as I can. I'll start as soon as I've put down the phone. If I can create the moulds tonight, I could get the resin into them tomorrow morning and start painting the eggs before I go to bed," Mr Landrow said, sounding excited. "They'd be ready to collect the day after tomorrow. Is this the telephone number to get you on?"

"Yes. Thank you, Mr Landrow." Twitch felt a rush of relief. "I don't know how much your eggs cost, but I've been saving my paper round wages and—"

"There'll be no charge," Mr Landrow said. "I'm happy to help. It would be wonderful to have spoonbills nesting in Briddvale."

Twitch didn't know what to say. "Thank you."

"I'll be in touch," Mr Landrow said. "And, Corvus, your grandad would have been proud of what you're doing."

Twitch ended the call and looked up at the clock. His mum's shift at the Elderberry Care Home didn't finish for another two hours. He would make himself a dinner of beans on toast and map out his plan. As he was heating his beans in the microwave, there was a knock at his front door. Opening it, he was surprised to see two police officers on the doorstep. One of them, Constable Greenwood, he knew. The other officer he recognized from Passerine Pike. It was Inspector Khan.

"Corvus Featherstone?" she asked.

"Yes. Hello, Constable Greenwood." Twitch smiled.

"I'm Inspector Khan," said the female officer.

"This is a bit delicate," Constable Greenwood said to Twitch, giving him an apologetic smile. "Is your mother home?"

An ice-cold jet of alarm froze Twitch's stomach as he realized Pippa's tin of eggs was sitting on his kitchen table. "What's this about?"

"I think it would be best if we came inside," Constable Greenwood said softly.

"Last Thursday, an egg thief targeted the nest of local peregrine falcons," Inspector Khan said, formally. "We have reason to believe that you may know something about these thefts." She gave him a meaningful look.

"Y-yes, I know about them," Twitch replied, feeling confused. "Did Ozuru and Terry come to the station and tell you about Jed Butler? We've been investigating him…"

"Are you investigating yourself?" Inspector Khan's face cracked into a patronizing smile.

"No!" Twitch felt his face flushing red with anger.

"We have a witness and evidence that place you at the scene of the crime."

"I … but … I would never steal birds' eggs." He looked pleadingly at Constable Greenwood. "You know that!"

"Then you won't mind if we come in and take a look around," Inspector Khan said, stepping through the doorway.

Twitch's heart was beating fast. "But … you can't think I took the eggs… I…"

"If you aren't hiding stolen eggs, there's nothing for you to get upset about, is there, Mr Featherstone?" Inspector Khan looked him dead in the eye and Twitch found himself stepping backwards to let her in.

Thinking fast, he showed them into the living room. Constable Greenwood sat down on the sofa. "Could you go and get Iris?" he asked. "Your mum should be here."

"She's at work."

"Oh! Do you know when she'll be back?"

Inspector Khan was looking around and, for the first time, Twitch realized just how many pictures of birds there were in his home. She sauntered over to the mantelpiece and picked up the fake guillemot's egg that was perched on a short dark wooden plinth.

"That's not real," Twitch said hurriedly. "It's made of resin."

"Twitch," Constable Greenwood said kindly. "We only have a few questions, if you're happy to answer them? Then we'll be on our way."

Twitch nodded but all he could think about was the tin of eggs on the kitchen table. He needed to get the lid on and hide it. "Would you like a cup of tea?" he asked, trying to smile.

They shook their heads, and his heart sank.

Inspector Khan pulled out a notepad. "Do you mind telling us where you were last Thursday afternoon and evening?"

Twitch perched on the edge of an armchair. "After school, I came home, dropped off my stuff, got changed, had tea, and went to Passerine Pike to watch the falcons." His voice was flat and resigned but his body was shaking. "I didn't go near the rocks. I watched from a distance."

"Would that be from the branches of a hawthorn

tree growing out of the fence that borders the Mord Estate?" Inspector Khan asked.

Twitch stiffened. He nodded, a growing sense of dread building in his chest.

"I see you like birds." Inspector Khan pointed her pen at the pictures on the walls. "And I'm led to believe you keep pigeons and chickens?"

"Yes." Twitch nodded.

"Where do your pigeons live?"

"On my bathroom roof."

"I'd love to see them. Would you mind showing us?" Inspector Khan asked.

As they filed out of the room, Twitch pulled at Constable Greenwood's sleeve and whispered urgently, "You know it wasn't me who stole those eggs. I wouldn't."

"I know. But my personal relationship with you is the reason why this isn't my case," he whispered. "You fit the suspect profile, Twitch, and there's evidence that places you at the scene of the crime."

Evidence! Twitch's heart clenched. What evidence could there be to make the police suspect him?

"This is a formality," Constable Greenwood continued. "If you cooperate with Inspector Khan, this will all be over soon. You mustn't worry."

Inspector Khan was already at the top of the stairs. Twitch hurried up, pushing past her into the bathroom.

"The birds are out here." Twitch climbed out of the open window, onto the flat roof, pointing at the pigeon loft he'd made from a wardrobe. "Actually. Would you mind if I quickly fed them?"

"Go ahead." Constable Greenwood nodded, poking his head out of the window.

Twitch unlatched the coop door and leaned in, so he couldn't be seen. Quickly he whipped a biro and a scrap of paper from his pocket and wrote:

J. Need help! Come! T.

Rolling the paper up between his thumb and forefinger, Twitch slid it into a metal capsule strapped to Frazzle's ankle and chased the bird out of the coop.

The dizzy pigeon flew in a circle around Twitch's head, then, realizing he had been liberated, climbed towards the purple sky above the orange blaze of the sunset and flew off in the direction of Aves Wood, where there was a bowl full of grain waiting. Twitch knew that Jack planned to return to the hide after following Jed Butler back to the campsite. He was going to wait there until Tara, Ava and Tippi came to do the night watch.

Twitch sent a silent prayer after Frazzle that Jack would get his message.

When he came back through the window, Inspector Khan was coming out of his mother's bedroom. "Is this your room?" she asked, pushing open his bedroom door. "Aha!" Striding to the iron mantel over the boarded-up fireplace, Inspector Khan pointed at Twitch's collection of broken swallows' eggs. "What have we here?"

"Broken eggshells," Twitch said. "They're from hatched swallow chicks." He pointed to a lumpen mud-and-straw mess clinging to the ceiling beside the open sash window. "Every year a family of swallows nest there. When the chicks hatch, the eggshells drop to the floor. I've collected them over the years. None of the shells come from whole eggs." He picked one up. "See?"

Inspector Khan eyed the broken bit of shell suspiciously. "Where are the swallows now then?"

"Migrating from Africa. They should arrive soon." Twitch looked to the window and wished he could sprout wings and fly out of it. He felt sick. What was he going to say when they found the tin?

"Anyone who knows the Featherstones," Constable Greenwood said, "knows about Twitch's swallows."

"Why aren't you questioning Jed Butler?" Twitch blurted out. "Birds' eggs didn't start going missing until he arrived in Briddvale. He has a previous record of stealing them."

"Jed Butler has been helping us with our enquiries," Inspector Khan replied. "What's that?" She pointed at the white cabin in the corner of the room.

"My bed," Twitch replied.

Inspector Khan pulled aside the curtain that covered the circular door into Twitch's bird-box bed and peered in. Wrinkling her nose, she withdrew, seemingly happy that there were no birds' eggs to be found in there.

As Twitch led the police downstairs, his heart was beating so fast he thought he might faint.

"I think we've seen enough to know Twitch isn't our egg thief, don't you, Inspector Khan?" Constable Greenwood said, giving Twitch a barely perceivable wink. He took a step in the direction of the front door.

A geyser of relief exploded in Twitch's chest. He smiled gratefully.

"Yes, I'll just pop my head into the kitchen and then we'll be off," Inspector Khan said, marching past him.

Twitch looked at Constable Greenwood in alarm and said, "They're not mine."

21
HINTS AND ALLEGATIONS

"Constable Greenwood," Inspector Khan called out, "it looks like we've found our egg thief!"

"I'm not the egg thief!" Twitch cried, running into the kitchen. "You have to believe me."

Inspector Khan was holding up Pippa's tin triumphantly.

"To whom do these eggs belong, Twitch?" Constable Greenwood asked sternly as he inspected them.

"I don't know!" Twitch replied honestly, and then, "I found them." He thought of telling the truth, but he'd made a promise to Pippa. A little too late, he realized he could have said they were his grandad's.

"Where did you find them?"

"Buried, in Aves Wood." The palms of his hands were sweating. He didn't like lying. He wasn't good at it. Inspector Khan narrowed her eyes as she weighed up this answer. Twitch's pulse was pounding in his temples. He felt like he might throw up.

"I'm afraid," Inspector Khan said, "I don't believe you. I think these are your eggs. Like the swallow eggs in your bedroom. And what is that?" She pointed to Twitch's rucksack, which he'd slung into the corner. It had his roll mat and sleeping bag strapped to it. "Been camping, have we?" She looked him dead in the eye. "I'll bet you were camping on Passerine Pike last Thursday night, weren't you?"

Twitch shook his head, shocked by what was happening.

"Twitch, we are going to have to assume the eggs are yours unless you can prove otherwise," Constable Greenwood said softly.

Twitch glared at him disbelievingly. The words stung. How could he think Twitch would steal an egg from a bird? After the cases he'd helped solve and the times he'd helped the police! He'd thought the constable knew him!

"Maybe young Corvus would be more talkative if we took him on a trip to the police station," Inspector Khan said in a threatening tone.

"I don't think..." Constable Greenwood started to say, but the doorbell rang. He stepped back so Twitch could open it. For a second Twitch thought it might be Jack, but Frazzle hadn't had enough time to fly to the hide, deliver his message and for Jack to get here.

"Hello, Twitch." It was Amita, his next-door neighbour. She smiled but he read concern in her brown eyes. "Did I see police officers on your doorstep? Oh! Yes! I did!" She pushed the door open and, without waiting for an invitation, bustled in, putting herself between Twitch and the officers. "To what does Twitch owe this pleasure?"

"We have reason to believe that Corvus Featherstone has been stealing birds' eggs," Inspector Khan said, holding up the tin of eggs. "He has been found in possession of a tin of at least twenty birds' eggs, which is a criminal offence."

Amita turned to look at Twitch. "Is that yours?"

Twitch shook his head.

"There. You have your answer. They're not his." She put her hand on Twitch's shoulder. "I have known this boy since the day he was born. He is no thief. And I'll tell you this" – she waggled a finger at them – "Twitch would steal from a human before he'd ever steal from a bird."

"He must come to the station for questioning," Inspector Khan insisted. She didn't like being undermined.

"Right now?" Amita's chin lifted.

"Er…" Inspector Khan's voice wavered. She glanced at Constable Greenwood, who shook his head.

"No. That's right." Amita leaned forward. "Twitch is a minor. The boy is thirteen. You cannot take him from his house to the police station without his parent or guardian present. His mother is working at the Elderberry Care Home and won't return until late this evening. I am an elderly neighbour, not a legal guardian, but if you ask me nicely, I'll let Iris know that you wish for her to bring Twitch to the police station tomorrow to answer your questions."

Inspector Khan's mouth opened and closed.

"Unless you can give me a very good reason why there is a problem with this arrangement, Twitch would like you both to leave his house immediately." She pulled Twitch to one side of the hall, leaving a clear exit path. "Wouldn't you, Twitch?"

Twitch nodded, worried that if he spoke, he'd break the spell Amita had cast on the officers.

"We'll be taking this as evidence." Inspector Khan jabbed the tin of eggs at Twitch as she walked past.

As the door shut, Twitch, who'd grown up with Amita as his adopted aunty, felt a fierce fire of love for her, which was followed by a wave of relief and gratitude. "Amita! You were brilliant." He hugged her. "Thank you!"

"Yes." Amita patted his back. "I was good, wasn't I?" She chuckled as she made her way to the kitchen. "Put the kettle on. You're going to tell me why those officers had hornets in their helmets."

Twitch explained about the peregrine falcons' stolen eggs and Jed Butler, why the officers wanted to question him, and how he'd come to have the mysterious tin of old eggs, although he avoided mentioning Pippa Bettany's name. "I don't know who the eggs belong to," he told her. "I was going to take the tin to the police station tomorrow. I think some of them are more than twenty years old."

"Well then you couldn't have stolen them!" Amita proclaimed triumphantly. "You weren't born when they were taken from their nests."

Twitch realized she was right and wished he'd thought of telling the officers that. It made him feel a bit better.

"You are a good boy." Amita slurped her tea. "You don't want a criminal record. It would harm your future. You must tell them about this bad Jed Butler."

"But they know about him!" Twitch frowned. "I don't understand why they suspect me!"

There came a frantic knocking on the front door.

Twitch opened it and Jack, Ava, Terry, Ozuru, Tippi and Tara all came tumbling through, looking worried.

"What's happening?" Jack asked. "We got your message."

"Are you OK?" Tara asked.

"We came as soon as we could," Terry said.

"The police were here," Twitch told them as he took them through to the kitchen. "They interrogated me."

"What?!" Ava cried out. She took Tippi's hand as her little sister moved close to her.

"Are you serious?" Terry asked.

Ozuru's mouth opened and closed like a goldfish.

"Oh, Twitch!" Tara gasped. "But why?"

"They think I'm the egg thief." The others gasped. "I fit the profile of an obsessed knowledgeable birdwatcher."

"That is true," Terry said and Ava punched his arm. "Ow!"

"But there's no evidence," Jack said. "They need proof."

"They say they have evidence that puts me at the scene of the crime. They thought my collection of cracked swallows' eggs was proof too."

"That's circumstantial," Jack protested as they swarmed into the kitchen. "Oh! Hello, Amita."

"I don't understand. Why aren't they going after Jed Butler?" Ava looked at Terry and Ozuru.

"We went to the police station and told them everything we know about him," Terry said to Twitch.

"The officer on the front desk wrote it all down," Ozuru said, "but they pointed out that we hadn't witnessed anything and didn't have proof to back up our allegations."

"I have to go to the police station tomorrow and answer questions," Twitch told them.

"They didn't cart you away in handcuffs," Terry pointed out. "That must be a good sign."

"Only because Amita was here." Twitch smiled gratefully at her. "She sent them packing."

"Amita, you're a legend!" Jack proclaimed and the others all agreed.

"Very true." She lifted her cup of tea and toasted herself.

"But it's not fair!" Tippi protested. "Twitch didn't do anything wrong."

"Life is never fair," Amita said, agreeing.

"If the police won't do it, we'll have to catch Jed Butler ourselves," Ava declared.

"We might be wrong about him, you know." Jack grabbed his rucksack. "I found something on my way back from Patchem's farm. An important clue!"

"A clue?" Twitch's spirits lifted.

"After following Jed and Henley, I came back through Aves Lock. That was where Pippa spied on us. I took a look around and found this." He put on his gloves and pulled out a blue tartan pencil case from his bag. "It was tucked under the bushes." He carefully unzipped it and emptied the contents onto the kitchen table.

Twitch saw nail scissors, tweezers, a scalpel, two thin silver rods that looked like dental tools, three empty plastic syringes with detached needles, and a small yellow plastic concertina device used for blowing air. "It's an egg-blowing kit!" he exclaimed in horror.

"Pippa's the egg thief!" Tippi exclaimed, shocked.

Twitch's mind was reeling. She had seemed so innocent and helpless when she'd brought him the tin of eggs. He'd thought she was protecting someone. He'd guessed it might be Mr Bettany. But could she really be the thief? He couldn't believe it.

"There's something else about Pippa you need to know," Twitch said, and he told them about her turning up with the tin of old eggs. "The police found them and took them away as evidence that I'm the thief."

"She framed you!" Ozuru gasped.

"But what about Jed Butler?" Terry said. "Are we crossing him off the suspect list?"

"No. We don't know that this is Pippa's." Jack pointed

to the egg-blowing kit. "All we know is that it belongs to the egg thief, and I found it near to where she was hiding to spy on us. It could belong to someone else."

"It doesn't look like the type of pencil case Jed Butler would buy," Tara observed.

"Where would Pippa Bettany get a syringe?" Ozuru said. "My dad's a doctor and I'm not allowed anywhere near his medical stuff."

They stared at the awful instruments.

"We can't take this to the police," Twitch said. "They'll think it's mine."

"If only we could catch the thief in the act," Tara said. "Then we'd know who it is."

"We can!" Twitch sat up straight, suddenly remembering the plan he'd had before the police had arrived. "I've thought of a way to catch the thief and protect the spoonbills at the same time."

"Tell us!" Jack said and they all leaned in.

"Remember that old nest in the willow tree on the east side of the pond? Well, it's given me an idea. We are going to turn it into a dummy spoonbill nest. A fake one."

"Why?" Tara frowned.

"We are going to rebuild the nest and put fake spoonbill eggs in it; lay a trap for the egg thief!"

"A sting operation!" Jack's eyes lit up. "Brilliant!"

"I called Mr Landrow, this artist that makes resin eggs. He's making a clutch of fake spoonbill eggs for the nest."

"What's a sting operation?" Tippi asked Ava.

"When you set up a tempting crime to catch a crook," she explained. "They take the bait. You catch them in the act. On go the handcuffs and off to prison they go."

"That *is* a good idea!" Tara said, her eyes glowing.

CAGED BIRD

When Twitch told his mum everything that had happened later that evening, her quiet dismay made him feel horrible.

"We're going straight to the police station in the morning to clear this up," Iris Featherstone said. "It is a misunderstanding. No one could think you'd do anything to harm a bird. It's a ridiculous notion."

"They say they have evidence," Twitch said. "I don't know what it is."

"It's always best to confront your problems head on," his mum said. "Otherwise they have a nasty habit of creeping up behind you and knocking you down. We'll get this sorted in the morning. You mustn't worry. Let's get an early night."

As he crawled into his cabin bed, Twitch felt alone and confused. Jack had decided to go with the girls to the hide, to plan the sting operation and watch over the spoonbills. Twitch wished he were there too. He pulled his duvet up to his chin and stared through the circular door in his bed, out through the window, wedged open for the swallows. Where were they?

When he awoke the next morning, a ball of fear was spinning in Twitch's stomach. It made him shiver and feel cold even though the sun was shining. He got dressed and went downstairs. His mum put a steaming bowl of porridge in front of him, but he wasn't hungry. He ate it to please her.

By the time they arrived at the police station, Twitch's nerves were making him breathe funny. He felt light-headed. He told himself it was stupid to feel frightened. He hadn't done anything wrong.

They were received by a duty officer. After a few minutes, Inspector Khan came out and introduced herself to Twitch's mum. She beckoned them through a door, along a grey corridor and into a bare room. It had a table with four chairs around it.

"Please, take a seat. I'll go get another officer to witness this voluntary interview."

Twitch and his mum sat down next to each other on one side of the table. His mum was trying to appear calm, but he could tell she was worried.

When Inspector Khan returned, she was carrying a cardboard box and was followed by a young officer with a shaving cut on his chin covered with a scrap of tissue.

"Thank you for coming in to help us with our enquiries," Inspector Khan said, putting the cardboard box on the floor and sitting down opposite them. "Are you happy for me to record this conversation?"

Twitch's mum looked at him. He nodded.

"Thank you." Inspector Khan took out a tablet from a drawer in the table, opened an audio recorder app and set it running. "It's twelve minutes past nine in the a.m. on the second of April. Present are Officer Seagrove, Iris Featherstone, Corvus Featherstone and Inspector Khan, who will be conducting this voluntary interview." She looked across the table. "Corvus, you have been asked to attend this interview because you are suspected of stealing four eggs from a peregrine falcon nest and destroying another, in the early hours of Friday the twenty-ninth of March. It is my duty to inform you that you are entitled to ask for a solicitor, and what you say here can be used in a court of law."

Twitch's mum frowned at this formal announcement. "A solicitor will not be necessary. There has been a mistake. Twitch did not take those eggs."

"Thank you." Inspector Khan reached down into the cardboard box. "I am showing the suspect Exhibit A." She lifted out Twitch's grandad's binoculars.

"Oh!" For a split second, Twitch was so relieved to see them, he smiled. Then it dawned on him, with a horrible jolt, that they were the evidence the police thought placed him at the scene of the crime.

"For the record, I'm holding up an old pair of binoculars. Corvus, do you recognize these?"

"Yes. They're mine. I lost them."

Inspector Khan placed them on the table in front of him. "Where did you lose them?"

"Passerine Pike."

"On the evening of Thursday the twenty-eighth of March?"

"No, the evening of Friday the twenty-ninth of March."

Inspector Khan frowned. "Where exactly on the pike did you lose them?"

"I don't know. I was using them to try to see the falcons' eggs, from the hawthorn tree, like you said. But on the Friday, not the Thursday. When I realized the eggs were gone, I was upset. I climbed down the tree and ran all the way to my friend Jack's house. You can ask him if you like. That's when I lost the binoculars. They must've fallen out of my pocket."

"Then can you explain to me how it was that these binoculars were handed in on Saturday morning as lost property. The person who found them said they'd discovered them on Friday morning, wedged into a rocky crevice at the top of the pike?"

Twitch's mouth dropped open. "That's not possible!" Inspector Khan looked blankly at him. "I didn't go near the peak." He turned to his mum. "I didn't!"

"Your friend, Ozuru Sawa, reported a second egg theft, of bullfinch eggs, on Sunday the thirty-first of March. Did you see those eggs?"

Twitch nodded.

"Did you steal the eggs?"

"No!"

"But you were in the area when the eggs disappeared?"

"I... I..." Twitch glared at Inspector Khan. "This is all wrong."

"There is a peregrine falcon egg and a bullfinch egg in that tin we found at your house, Corvus."

"That tin," his mum snapped, "isn't Twitch's."

"If you knew anything about birds' eggs," Twitch said angrily, "you'd see that those eggs are really old! Older than me. There's a golden oriole egg in there. They haven't bred in this country since before I was born!" Anger was coursing through his veins. "Show them to an expert, they'll tell you."

"I see you know your collection well," Inspector Khan replied with a smile. "Don't you think it would be better for your poor mum if you came clean and just admitted to taking the eggs? It'll be better for you in the long run."

Something inside Twitch snapped. He found he was on his feet with his hands flat on the table, leaning towards Inspector Khan. "No! I don't think it would be better to own up to a crime I would NEVER commit!" He could hear he was shouting but he couldn't stop himself. He was so angry. "You think I'm the egg thief, but you know nothing. Nobody my age would steal a bird's egg. It has to have been an older person. We *children*" – he spat the word at her – "know that the wildlife of the world is under threat. More and more animals and birds become extinct every year. We are frightened for the planet. I'm scared of what is waiting in my future. I want it to be filled with plants and insects and billions of beautiful birds, but will it? No, because habitats are shrinking, the climate is warming, weather systems are changing, and humans are cruel. I would NEVER steal a bird's egg. Every egg is a bird that this planet needs. Those empty eggshells in that tin are tiny empty graves. An egg in a bird's nest is life and hope for the future. I have been doing everything I can to protect them. I will NOT admit to doing something I would *never* do!" The words rushed out of him like a torrent, leaving him feeling empty and light-headed. He folded his arms and sat back down, determined not to say another word.

His mother was looking at him proudly. She turned and glared at Inspector Khan. "I think you have your answer."

"There's one more thing I would like Corvus to do, if you don't mind," Inspector Khan said to both of them. "We have a witness who says they saw a boy matching your description up by the falcon nest on Thursday evening. We'd like to put you in a line-up and see if they can positively identify you." She cocked her head, wearing an insincere smile. "If, as you say, you would never steal a bird's egg, I'm sure you won't mind remaining here to take part in the line-up?"

A witness? Twitch's heart fluttered anxiously. How could there be a witness when he was never there?

"Of course he doesn't mind," his mother was saying. "Then you'll see you've got the wrong boy."

23
HIDE AND SEEK

Jack opened his eyes. He was alarmingly close to Terry, whose sleeping bag was pulled so tightly around his face that he resembled a navy-blue larva. Light filtered through the cracks in the tepee and he could see his own breath. It was early.

After they'd left Twitch's, everyone was on edge. They'd decided to stick together and all stay in the hide to watch over the spoonbills. It made them feel like they were doing something. Jack wondered how Ozuru was faring, up in the crow's nest.

Carefully and quietly, Jack wriggled out of his sleeping bag. He crawled from the tent-shaped room into the tepee, and stood up, stretching out his stiff muscles.

"Morning," Ava whispered, her head poking out of Ozuru's pop-up tent, which he'd assembled in the cabin for the girls. "I was wondering when someone would wake up."

"Couldn't you sleep?"

"No. I kept thinking about Twitch having to go to the police station today."

"I know." Jack nodded. "Me too."

"I hope he's OK."

"Twitch is the strongest person I've ever met," Jack said. "He'll be fine. The police have got it wrong. They'll soon see that." But Jack wasn't sure what to think. His mind felt like an enormous machine with turning cogs, pipes ejecting steam, and screens scrolling data. He was angry on Twitch's behalf. Everyone in Briddvale knew Twitch would never hurt a bird! But he also understood that the police had a procedure to follow. He'd been trying to follow one himself.

"You don't think that Twitch *is* the egg thief, do you?" Terry said, sitting up. "He does match the profile."

"Don't be an idiot." Jack shoved him back down.

"Ouch! I was only joking!"

"Yeah, well, don't." Jack gritted his teeth. He wasn't really cross with Terry. He was angry with himself for not solving the case yet.

"Do you think Twitch is scared?" Tara's soft voice said, her head appearing beside Ava's in the door of their tent.

"I would be," Tippi said, wriggling between the older girls.

"He's innocent. The police will see that," Jack said with a confidence he didn't feel. "Now, let's get dressed. We've got a sting operation to prepare and a thief to catch."

"Let's make Twitch proud," Tara said, getting up.

"Can we have breakfast first?" Ava asked. "I'm starving."

"Ozuru's brought everything we need for a fry-up," Terry said. "Including a frying pan."

"Did someone say my name?" Ozuru said, climbing down the ladder.

"There is one advantage of Twitch not being here," Terry said. "I won't feel guilty about eating bacon and sausages."

"Oh really?" Tara gave him a hard stare. "I don't eat meat either."

"Yeah." Terry smiled. "But you don't look sad when I eat it."

The Twitchers sprang into action, storing their bedding in the tent-shaped room, clearing the shed for the day's work. Jack put the pencil case containing the egg-blowing kit into a freezer bag and hung it from a nail on their case wall. Ozuru set up his little gas camping stove in front of the hide and set about cooking eggs, beans, tomatoes, bacon and sausages.

The pond water reflected the cloudless pale sky like a scarred and spotted old mirror. Jack went to the water's edge, wondering if the spoonbills would come out for their breakfast. Aves Wood exerted its power over him, slowing his whirling mind and quietening his anxious heart. He needed to be methodical, to consider the evidence they had and all the suspects. He thought Twitch's sting operation was a good idea, but it bothered him that he was yet to solve the case. It would be better if they knew who they expected to see robbing their phoney nest.

"Jack, breakfast!" Ava called.

Breakfast was a silent affair. Everybody was preoccupied with their thoughts and their stomachs. Jack was mopping up his egg yolk with a crust of bread when he heard a voice, nervous and high, calling, "Twitch? Twitch. Are you there?"

Glancing at the others, he rose from his tree stump and whispered, "I'll deal with this."

As he came out of the hide, he saw Pippa Bettany go rigid. Every muscle in her body looked ready for flight. "Twitch isn't here," he told her.

She looked past him to the door of the hide. "I need to speak with him. It's urgent."

"You'll have to go to the police station."

"What?" Pippa gasped.

"That's where Twitch is. The police searched his house yesterday and found a tin of eggs. Know anything about them?" Pippa's hands flew to her pale face. "Twitch is at the police station this morning, being interviewed. They think he's the egg thief!"

"Oh, no!" Pippa cried, turned and bolted.

"Wait!" Jack called after her. He needed to ask her about the egg-blowing kit and where she'd got the eggs. He glanced back over his shoulder at the hide, then made a snap decision and sprinted after her.

He was in such a hurry that when he emerged onto the footpath, he didn't pause to check the coast was clear. He burst through the wall of ferns and almost collided with a woman. She let out an alarmed cry and staggered back.

"Sorry," he called over his shoulder, as he dashed away.

He saw the burgundy hat and realized he'd almost knocked over Mrs Drake. She was staring after him, looking stunned, but Jack didn't have time to linger. He had to find out who Pippa was running to. It could be the egg thief.

Pippa ran clumsily, suggesting to Jack that she was

upset. She kept shaking her head as if arguing with herself. When she reached her grandad's shop, she hurled herself through the door.

Jack hung back, sidling up to the window and peeping through. He could see the back of Pippa's head. She was gesturing wildly with her hands. Mr Bettany was behind the counter. He looked taken aback. He lifted the wooden top to let her through. Pippa turned and Jack saw tears on her cheeks. Mr Bettany looked over his granddaughter's head, speaking to someone that Jack couldn't see. Opening the door into the back of the shop, he ushered Pippa through and the two of them disappeared. A matronly woman took up the post of cashier.

After a minute, Jack went in. He browsed the sweets with his hands in his pockets, trying to act casual. He strained his ears, but couldn't hear anything from the back room. Picking up a packet of chocolate biscuits and a bag of toffees, he went to the counter. "Hi." He smiled brightly as the woman rang up the biscuits and sweets on the till. "Didn't I see Pippa run in a moment ago?" He looked around. "She looked upset."

"Mr Bettany's granddaughter? She's got herself in a bit of a state. I don't know what it's about." The woman lowered her voice, peering over her glasses. "She's an excitable girl that one. Yesterday she went haring out of here holding an old tin in front of her like it was a bomb about to go off!" She shook her head. "I think she's lonely. She doesn't seem to have many friends."

Jack put the biscuits in his coat pocket and thanked the woman, opening the bag of toffees as he left the shop. So, the eggs that had got Twitch into trouble were Mr Bettany's! Unwrapping a toffee, he put it in his mouth as he strolled back along the Briddvale Road mulling this news over. He'd never have guessed the newsagent was an egger! Was he also the thief? Mr Bettany had been up at the pike the night the eggs were stolen. He stopped walking. Had Pippa Bettany discovered her grandad's egg-blowing kit and accidentally dropped it by Aves Lock when she'd been spying on them? It was possible. How else had it got there? He strolled on. Had Pippa brought the eggs to Twitch yesterday to set him up on purpose? He shook his head. No, she had looked genuinely shocked and upset when she'd realized Twitch was in trouble. Still, he'd only get answers by interviewing her. Immediately he knew that it was something that Tara would do better than him. He resolved to talk to her about it when he got back to the hide.

When he reached the canal, Jack saw Merle Drake

fishing. He looked around for Evelyn, aware that he owed her an apology for barging past her, but there was no sign of her, so he slipped by, unseen, and ambled through the car park to the gate and into the woods.

"You're back!" came Tara's voice from behind him. Jack turned as Tara and Tippi appeared carrying bundles of sticks in their arms. "We are collecting materials for the fake nest."

"I've got lots of moss in my rucksack," Tippi told him.

"I can help," Jack said. "I've brought chocolate biscuits and toffees to give us energy."

"Yay!" Tippi cheered as he offered her a toffee.

While helping to gather sticks for the nest, Jack told Tara and Tippi what he'd discovered at the newsagent's. "I was thinking that we should question Pippa. Maybe you two would be better at doing it than me. You're less scary."

"I don't mind doing it," Tara replied. "I like Pippa. She's sweet. I'm sure she doesn't want to hurt anyone."

"Hmm," Jack replied, picking up a handful of twigs. "I'm not."

Once they had enough nest building materials, they headed back towards the hide. Emerging onto the footpath, they found themselves face to face with two police officers. One was carrying a duffle bag.

"Morning," Jack greeted them cheerfully, pleased to see the police were patrolling the woods.

The two officers nodded as they passed.

Ava, Terry and Ozuru were out on the water in the boat. They dumped their sticks in a pile outside the hide and Tara climbed the ladder to the walkway and waved at the dinghy. Jack held up the biscuits and signalled that they should come ashore.

On his way inside, Jack stumbled. Looking down, he noticed a dark patch of soil in the tepee floor. The ground was uneven and looked like it had been turned over by a trowel.

"What did they do to the floor?" he wondered aloud, stamping it down flat so it wouldn't trip anyone else.

"Jack," Tara called down from the walkway. "Frazzle is still in the coop. Do you think we should release him? I'm not very good at picking up the pigeons."

"Gosh. Yes. I forgot all about poor Frazzle. Don't worry, I'll take care of him." Jack climbed up to the coop and opened the door of the dog crate. He gently corralled Frazzle into a corner and cupped his hands around the bird. It had taken him months to learn how to pick up Twitch's pigeons without jumping or freaking out, but now he enjoyed doing it. Frazzle *corrruurr*-ed at him before opening his wings and flying up over the still waters of the pond, wheeling around and disappearing in the direction of Twitch's house.

He watched Ava and Ozuru jump out of the boat, followed by a hesitant Terry, who helped them pull the dinghy out of the pond. As they laid the cover over it, Jack went down to the cabin.

"So that's where you went," Terry said, stuffing his hand in the toffee bag and taking two. "The sweet shop!"

"Today, I think we should split into two groups," Jack said, ushering everyone into the cabin. They sank onto their tree stumps with serious expressions. "One will build the fake nest, the other will watch our main suspects in case they get itchy fingers and try to steal an egg."

Tippi's hand shot up. "I want to build the nest."

"Me too," Tara said.

"I would like to help with the nest," Ozuru said.

"OK, so me, Ava and Terry will tail our suspects."

"Henley and Jed will either be fishing or at the campsite," Ava said.

"We should take a walk along the towpath," Terry said. "If we don't spot them, go up to Patchem's farm."

"Sounds good to me," Ava said.

"Well hold on a minute," Jack said. "Are we sure

they're our main suspects? I think we should go over the case. To summarize…"

"Fings ah goin berry badvee?" Terry said with a mouthful of toffee.

Jack ignored him. "Our prime suspect is Jed Butler. A known egg collector, with a conviction. He has climbing gear. He's strong. He's knowledgeable about birds."

"He's not nice," Tippi added.

"That's not evidence," Ava said.

"I didn't like the way he talked to Twitch," Tippi said. "It was mean."

"I think it's Henley Brandy," Ava said. "You all saw how angry he got when he didn't win on Monday. He's weird enough to collect eggs. Twitch saw him up on the pike the night of the theft and he was obviously burying something with that spade. I'll bet it was a box containing the stolen eggs."

"I still think it's Jed," Terry said.

"I'd like us to consider Pippa Bettany," Jack said. "After I told her about Twitch being at the police station she ran straight to her grandad. That tin of eggs is his, I'm sure of it."

"What!" Terry choked on his own spit and had a coughing fit.

"They were up on the pike the night of the theft," Jack went on. "He is obviously a collector. He could be our thief. He might even have framed Twitch."

"Mr Bettany!" Tara looked shocked. "I would never have thought in a million years he would do something like that! That can't be true!"

"Pippa could have dropped his egg-blowing kit when she was spying on us." He pointed at their case wall.

"Hang on. Where is it?" Ava asked. "Has one of you moved it?"

Jack spun around to look. The nail from which he'd hung their biggest clue was empty.

"It's gone!" Ozuru gasped.

24
SCRAMBLED

Thoughts streaked through Jack's brain like speeding traffic. He couldn't hear them over the hammering of his own heart. Someone had been in the hide! Was it the egg thief? It couldn't have been Pippa Bettany. Unless she'd led him away on purpose! Had Jed Butler or Henley Brandy snuck in here while he and the others were in the boat or collecting sticks?

There was an explosion of alarmed chatter as everyone talked at once.

"We mustn't panic," Jack said, holding up his hands for quiet, trying to unscramble his own thoughts.

"What if the egg thief is listening?" Tippi sounded frightened.

"I don't get it. Who could have come in and taken it?" Ava wondered.

"The only people I saw in the woods this morning

were police officers…" Jack fell silent, remembering the black duffle bag they'd been carrying.

"You don't think…" Terry looked alarmed.

"They'll think the egg-blowing kit was ours!" Ava's voice was a squeak.

"Worse." Jack could barely breathe. "They might think it belongs to Twitch!" He had been trying to keep a clear head, to push down his emotions so he could be a good detective, but the overwhelming feeling that he was failing his best friend hit him like a tsunami. The thief was running rings around them, always one step ahead. He felt certain the egger was the one who'd set up Twitch.

"What are we going to do?" Tara said, looking tearful.

"We stick to the plan," Jack said, thumping his fist down on the table. "It's the only thing we can do. Twitch's idea is a good one."

"We're going to get that evil sucker," Terry said vehemently, "if it's the last thing we do."

"For the lost falcons, for the spoonbills and for Twitch," Jack said, giving The Twitchers Salute. Everyone answered with a salute of their own. "Let's go."

"When we catch the thief," Tippi said to Tara as they got up from the table, "I'm going to kick him in the shins."

Ava, Terry and Jack waved goodbye to the others and set off through Aves Wood to hunt for their suspects.

"Bingo," Jack whispered. "Look! Henley Brandy! Coming towards the gate."

"Quick, act natural," Terry hissed, lifting his binoculars and looking around frantically.

"Morning," Henley called out to them. He nodded at the gate. "Mind opening that for me?" He was carrying a digging fork and a tackle box. "Got my hands full."

Ava helped him through the kissing gate.

"What are you digging for?" Jack asked. "Treasure?"

"Treasure to me," Henley said, "and the fish."

"Worms?" Terry guessed.

"Some worms. Some beetle larvae."

"Ooh, can we see?" Jack said, feigning interest. "Did you get any juicy ones?"

"I did." Henley beamed at Jack, putting his tackle box down. "I don't chop worms up like the others do. I reckon whole worms are more tempting for a fish. Bigger, ain't they?"

"You must hate birds," Jack ventured.

"Can't say I hate any part of nature. What makes you think I'd hate birds?"

"Competition for the worms," Jack said. "They eat them too."

"Birds are useful actually. They know where the best worms are. They help me find my bait."

"Do you look for their nests?" Ava asked.

"I look to see where they're circling and landing. That's where I dig. It doesn't always work, mind. The other day there were birds up at Passerine Pike. I tried to dig for worms there, but the ground was too rocky. Full of flints. I found nothing but thread-thin wrigglers and a few beetles. I've been digging in Farmer Patchem's top field all morning. I got a good haul." He crouched down and opened his tackle box, pulling trays open like a fan, revealing compartments containing fishing line and colourful flies. The body of the tackle box had slim drawers. Jack leaned down to see what Henley kept inside. "Check out these beauties." Henley pulled a tub from one of the compartments, opening it to reveal a writhing spaghetti of worms. "One of these boys is going to catch me a big fish tomorrow." His sandy eyebrows lifted in anticipation of the great moment.

"Do you like eggs?" Terry asked.

"Eggs?" Henley frowned at this odd question. "No. I don't eat 'em. Used to bring me out in hives as a kid. Think I might be allergic."

"No, I mean, like blowing them and collecting the shells," Terry elaborated.

Henley look genuinely perplexed. "What would I want to do that for? Tha's weird."

"I saw Mr Drake fishing down by Crowther Bridge," Jack said, steering the conversation back to fishing. "He's got a special bait recipe, you know?"

"Merle fishes every minute he can. Loves it. Evelyn, bless her, has to occupy herself or sit there beside him."

"What does she do if he's fishing all day?" Ava asked.

"Rambling, she says." Henley chuckled. "Told me yesterday that quite a few of her long walks take her past tea shops and clothing boutiques. She's proper friendly is Evelyn; although, whatever you do, don't touch her hat. I asked if I could try it on the other day and she nearly bit my head off. It belonged to her dead father, you see. She loves it."

Jack remembered Twitch telling him something similar, about trying to pick up Mrs Drake's hat and her snatching it, and he nodded. He wondered why she wouldn't let anyone touch it.

"It was unlucky what happened with your bait and that boat," Terry said.

"Phil says I drove the fish into Dr Sawa's nets with my bad music, but I read this article, see, and it said that fish and plants like music."

"Maybe you're playing them the wrong music," Ava suggested helpfully.

"What were you playing?" Terry asked, curious.

"Mozart," Henley said, as if it were obvious. "Phil said that Dr Sawa only won yesterday 'cause of me and Mozart, and that it should of been him who won with Mrs Crocker." He sighed. "He's pretty cross with me."

"That's not very sportsmanlike," Terry said.

"Oh, Phil's all right, just obsessed with winning. Don't think of nothing else. The person I have difficulties getting along with is Jed." Jack was suddenly listening intently. "One of the things I like about fishing is the people you get to pass the time of day with, but not him. He's difficult. I can't get a conversation out of him."

"Is he fishing today?" Jack asked.

"I haven't seen him along the canal," Henley said, "but he left the campsite early, so he must be."

25

BANNED!

"I don't think Henley Brandy is our thief," Jack said, as they came out beside the canal. "I'm dropping him to the bottom of the suspect list."

"What now?" Ava asked.

"You two find Jed Butler. Watch him like a hawk." Jack was walking so fast he was almost running; something Henley said had triggered a chain reaction in his head. "I need to talk to Twitch."

"About what?" Terry asked.

"I'll be back as soon as I can," Jack called over his shoulder, as he sprinted away.

On his way up Twitch's road, Jack saw Pam and Clem standing in front of two police cars parked outside Twitch's house. A cold flash of fear made him catch his breath. "What's going on?" he demanded as Pam came towards him.

"Haven't you heard?" Pam said. "Twitch is the thief who stole those eggs from the falcons' nest! The police are searching his house. They have a warrant and everything."

"What?" The news hit Jack like a blow.

"Hey, could we interview you about being the accused's best friend?" Pam smiled sweetly. "The police won't talk to me."

The door of Twitch's house was open. Jack saw Inspector Khan and another officer standing in the doorway. He pushed past Pam; he had to know what was going on.

"Quick, film him," Pam hissed to Clem.

Jack darted into Twitch's front garden to a spot where he couldn't be seen, and stealthily crept towards the open door.

"We didn't find anything new," the officer was saying.

"It doesn't matter," said Inspector Khan. "We have his egg collection in the two tins and the witness testimony. It's enough to charge him."

Jack couldn't believe what he was hearing. He stumbled forward. "Where's Twitch?" he demanded.

"Corvus Featherstone is at the police station," Inspector Khan replied tartly, narrowing her eyes as she looked at him.

"He's innocent!"

"Your friend," Inspector Khan said, pushing past him, "has been positively identified by a witness who saw him by the falcon nest last Thursday night." She marched to one of the police cars. "He will be charged this afternoon." She got in and shut the door.

"No!" Jack cried out. "You can't do this! Twitch is not a thief!" He slammed his hands on the bonnet of the car. "You've got to listen to me!"

A severe look from the officer driving and a rev of the engine made Jack step back. As the cars disappeared down the road, he dropped to the kerb, letting his head fall into his hands. What was happening? Who was this witness who'd said they'd seen Twitch by the falcon nest? It was a lie! And what had Inspector Khan meant when she'd said they had his collection in the *two* tins? Where had the second one come from? Jack's insides were churning. Twitch had told him that egg collectors were ruthless, but framing a child for a crime he didn't commit? That was indefensible.

Twitch was in serious trouble. Jack had to do something. He saw his friend's bike lying on his front lawn. Jumping to his feet, Jack grabbed it, threw his leg over the saddle and raced after the police cars.

"Follow him!" he heard Pam shout.

When he got to the police station, Jack jumped off

the bike, chucking it into the bike rack at the front of the building. He sprinted up the ramp, bursting through the double doors.

"Jack!" Constable Greenwood was standing behind the counter at the front desk. "I thought you might turn up."

"Constable Greenwood! Twitch would never..." He was gasping for breath. "It's not him! It's Martin Shrike, or Jed Butler, or whatever his name is!"

"Jack, this isn't my case. It's Inspector Khan's." Constable Greenwood's expression was annoyingly understanding. "A witness has come forward saying they saw a boy that matches Twitch's description, up by the nest, on the night the eggs were stolen. They've picked him out from a line-up."

"But that's not true!" Jack cried. "It's a lie!"

"Were you there?"

"No, but..." Jack stared at the expression on Constable Greenwood's face and could see that Twitch was in serious trouble. "What about Jed Butler?"

"We know about Jed Butler's past. He served his time and has paid the penalty for his crimes. He works for a bird charity now, ringing, collecting data and protecting birds. They've vouched for him. He's actually been very helpful to the investigation."

"You can't believe that?"

"As a matter of fact," Constable Greenwood said, "I do."

"The eggs only started going missing when he came to Briddvale!"

"Let it go, Jack."

"You believe a stranger over Twitch?"

"Calm down." Constable Greenwood came out from behind the counter and gestured to a plastic chair along the wall. "Take a seat."

"What's going to happen to him?" Jack threw himself into the chair in utter despair. "Will he go to prison?"

"Nothing like that," Constable Greenwood said in a reassuring voice. "If Inspector Khan believes she has enough evidence, she will charge him."

"Then what?"

"There will be a trial..."

"Could he be sent to prison?"

"It will be a youth court, with a judge..."

"But what if he's found guilty?"

"It's a first offence and he's a minor. If the judge is fair, he'll get a Youth Conditional Caution..."

"Is that a criminal record?"

"It's a formal warning with conditions. Corvus may have to do some community work" – Constable Greenwood looked away – "and he may have to stay away from certain types of places."

"Why are you calling him Corvus all of a sudden?" Jack snapped. He could feel the veins in his forehead bulging, he was so angry. "He's Twitch!" He wanted to scream at the unfairness of the whole situation. Twitch had done nothing wrong!

"Jack, simmer down," Constable Greenwood said softly.

"What are these two tins?" Jack demanded. "Inspector Khan said Twitch had a collection in two tins…"

"She told you that?"

"Those tins aren't Twitch's."

"One tin was found in Twitch's kitchen. I saw it myself. The second" – he paused – "is a Tupperware container. It was found this morning buried inside your hide. There were three eggs inside and a sweet pastry."

"What?" Jack was so shocked, his anger sluiced away. "In our hide?" A memory of churned-up soil in the tepee-room floor flashed into his mind. Someone had been into the hide to plant evidence to frame Twitch! The same person must have taken the egg-blowing kit from the case wall. He thought carefully before asking his next question. "But you haven't found any egg-blowing stuff, have you?" Jack studied Constable Greenwood's eyes.

"No, Jack, but the eggs are enough. It's illegal to own them."

"How did your officers know to look in the hide?" Jack asked. "Were they tipped off?"

"I … er … I don't know," Constable Greenwood said, his eyes dropping to the floor. Jack felt like he was avoiding the question. "Like I said. This is not my case."

So, the thief had discovered their hide, taken back their egg-blowing kit and planted three eggs in Tara's Tupperware and buried it in the floor of the hide to frame Twitch. All they'd had to do was call the police, and they'd come along and dug it up, thinking they had further proof that Twitch was the egger! Jack's insides crackled with indignation.

"Don't look like that, Jack. Twitch is under suspicion, but this is a process. If he's innocent, it will become clear."

"He *is* innocent," Jack growled, glaring at Constable Greenwood. After all Twitch had done to help the police last year, finding the bank robbery money, and stopping the illegal hunting of birds of prey, Constable Greenwood should know better. "I'm going to wait here until Twitch comes out," Jack said, pulling his notebook from his pocket, "and work on solving the mystery of who the *real* thief is."

Constable Greenwood sighed and nodded, returning to the front desk.

After half an hour, the double doors opened, and Ava, Tippi, Tara, Ozuru and Terry filed into the police station looking worried.

"Is it true Twitch has been arrested?" Tippi's bottom lip trembled.

"We saw Pam," Ava said. "She came and told us."

"Don't worry, Tippi," Jack reassured her. "Twitch is just answering questions and helping the police." He glanced over at Constable Greenwood. "Let's go outside." Jack opened his arms to usher them back through the door.

The Twitchers huddled together in front of the police station.

"Someone has set Twitch up," Jack said, keeping his voice low. "This morning, three birds' eggs were found in your Tupperware, Tara, buried in the floor of the hide."

"What! When?" Ava asked.

"It must've happened when we were collecting sticks, and you" – he gestured to Terry, Ozuru and Ava – "were out in the boat." There was a murmur of dismay. "I think the thief found our hide, saw our case wall with their egg-blowing kit on it and panicked. They must've taken their kit back, put the eggs into Tara's Tupperware…"

"It was sitting on the table," Tara said.

"Then they buried the container in the tepee floor, and tipped off the police. Constable Greenwood showed no knowledge of an egg-blowing kit existing, so I don't think the police have it. Which means…"

"The thief has it," Terry finished his sentence.

"If he's discovered the hide, with the crime wall and his egg-blowing kit…" Ava's eyes were wide. "Jed Butler knows we're on to him."

"Here's the strange thing," Jack said. "The police are certain it's not him. Constable Greenwood says he works for a bird charity."

"Doesn't mean he's innocent," Ozuru said.

"You don't think Jed Butler is our thief?" Ava asked him.

"Then it has to be Mr Bettany!" Terry said.

"But he was in his shop this morning." Jack shook his head. "I saw him. It would've been almost impossible for him to get to the hide and make the call in time."

"It feels like we're fighting against an invisible villain," Ozuru said glumly.

"That's what fighting evil always feels like," Ava told him.

They all turned at the sound of the police station door opening.

"Twitch!" Jack exclaimed.

Iris Featherstone drew back so that Twitch could talk with his friends. They gathered protectively around him.

"Are you OK?"

"What did they say to you?"

"Are you in trouble?"

"I can't believe they think you did it!"

"I'm all right," Twitch said in a muted voice, his hands firmly wedged in his pockets. "The chairman of the Aves Wood Wildlife Committee is in there." He glanced back over his shoulder.

"Mr Allen?" Jack said, studying Twitch's pale face with concern. "What does he want?"

"I'm not allowed into Aves Wood until the court case is over," Twitch said blankly. "If I'm found guilty, he says I'll be banned for life."

They all gasped and Jack's mind reeled. There couldn't be a worse punishment for Twitch.

"Everyone thinks I'm the egg thief," Twitch said with a defeated shrug. "Nothing I could say would convince them I'm not. They found three unblown birds' eggs buried in the hide." He looked at them all. "They think they're mine. One of the peregrine falcon eggs was in there." His head drooped. "It was so sad to see it. It was so cold."

"Twitch, someone is framing you," Ava said.

"It's the real thief," Jack said.

"But you mustn't worry," Tara told him. "We're going to catch them and clear your name."

"You guys are the best," Twitch said. "But … you may not want to be my friends much longer—"

"Don't say that," Jack cut him off.

"Mr Allen and the police are talking about bulldozing the hide." Twitch's voice was almost a whisper.

"What?!"

"No!"

"They can't!"

"Listen to me," Jack asserted forcefully. "That isn't going to happen. We've got your plan, Twitch. The sting. Whoever is doing this knows we're on to them. They're panicking. They've had to give up three of their precious eggs to try and get us out of the way, but that's their big mistake."

"If they've been to the hide" – Twitch looked at Jack – "do you think they've seen the spoonbills?"

"I don't know," Jack's stomach lurched, "but we don't have time to stand around feeling sorry for ourselves; we've got to catch that thief to protect the birds and clear your name!"

26

CACKLEFART COLLECTOR

"Terry, Ozuru, you go back to the hide and keep watch from the crow's nest," Jack said. "I want you to keep a log of every human you see in Aves Wood."

"I've made the nest," Tippi told Twitch. "It's in the hide."

"It's really good," Tara said enthusiastically. "We used your book. It looks exactly like a spoonbill nest."

"It's got moss in it and everything," Tippi said proudly.

"I haven't had time to call Mr Landrow back." Twitch looked across at his mum. "Mum, do you think you could drive me and my friends to Peter Landrow's house tomorrow morning?"

"Peter Landrow? Gosh, I haven't heard that name in a long time." She looked surprised. "Why are you visiting him?"

"We've got a plan to prove I'm not the egg thief. We need a few of Mr Landrow's fake eggs to pull it off."

"Yes, of course I'll drive you. It'll be nice to see Dad's old friend. But" – she glanced back at the police station – "let's get out of here. I want to go home."

"We didn't eat any lunch," Tara said. "I'm going to take the girls back to mine to eat."

"I'm starving," Tippi said.

"We'll bring food back for you," Ava said to Terry and Ozuru.

"We'll make sure the spoonbills are safe, Twitch," Tara assured him. "Don't you worry."

"Come over after breakfast tomorrow," Twitch said. "We can go to Mr Landrow's and collect the fake spoonbill eggs. You'll like him, Tippi. He's a great egg artist."

"Can I come with you now?" Jack asked, and Twitch nodded.

They put Twitch's bike in the back of the car and drove to the Featherstone home in silence. In his head, Jack went over what he knew about each of the suspects, trying to work out who could've framed his friend. When they reached Twitch's house, one of them, Mr Bettany, was on the doorstep, ringing the bell.

A look of relief crossed Mr Bettany's face when he saw Twitch get out of the car. "I heard you were at the police station."

"Have you come to sack me?" Twitch asked.

"Sack you?" Mr Bettany appeared puzzled by this question.

"From the paper round," Twitch said. "For being a thief."

"But you're not a thief, Twitch." Mr Bettany blinked. "You're possibly one of the most honest boys I've ever employed. You've never even so much as swiped a bag of sweets from the counter when I wasn't looking. No. I'm not going to fire you."

Iris Featherstone beamed at the newsagent. "Would you like to come in for a cup of tea?" she asked him warmly.

"If that would be OK." He looked at Twitch. "There's something I need to talk to you about."

They went through to the kitchen.

Mr Bettany removed his flat cap and twisted it nervously in his hands as he sat down at the kitchen table. "Twitch, I need to confess something." The words hurried out of him. "The tin of birds' eggs Pippa brought to you. They're mine." His head bowed. "I fear they've landed you in a lot of trouble."

"I thought they must be," Twitch told him. "They were too old for her to have collected them."

Mr Bettany looked ashamed. "When I was a lad, collecting birds' eggs was a thing you did if you loved being outdoors, along with hunting for fossils or catching and pinning butterflies. These days those hobbies are illegal or frowned upon, and with good reason." He sighed. "Times have changed."

"They certainly have," Iris agreed.

"My dad loved to take me out watching birds and collecting eggs. It was something he did when he was a lad." Mr Bettany reached out and lifted a chicken egg from a clay bowl in the centre of the table. "Cacklefarts, he used to call them." He smiled sadly. "Said it was on account of the noise hens made when they were laying." He looked at Twitch. "He'd say, 'Son, let's go cacklefart collecting.'" He shook his head. "I kept that tin of eggs, not because I care for the shells much really, but because each egg is a container for a memory of my father."

Twitch's expression softened and Jack guessed that Mr Bettany's father was dead.

"We only ever took one egg from a nest. Never a whole clutch." He sounded boyish, defending his actions. "I stopped collecting eggs once I got to an age when learning to drive and meeting young women became more interesting." He glanced at Iris and blushed a little. "That tin has been sitting in my loft for fifty years. I didn't know that Pippa had found it."

"I think she was worried that you'd be accused of being the egg thief and get arrested," Twitch said.

"Yes. I can see that. I like taking Pippa to spot birds, like my father did with me. She and I were up at Passerine Pike looking at the peregrine falcons the evening the eggs were stolen. When Pippa heard about the theft, she became distressed and frightened. She's played in my loft countless times. She has a den up there. I didn't know she'd found the tin. She was scared the police would knock on my door, find the eggs and haul me off to jail."

"That's why she brought the tin to me," Twitch said.

"I am not the egg thief," Mr Bettany said.

"I know that." There was a hint of humour in Twitch's expression. "If you were, your whole loft would be full of eggs, and you wouldn't let Pippa up there."

"She thinks the world of you, Twitch." Mr Bettany smiled at him. "You've always been kind to her in the shop, not like the other newspaper round kids. I've seen her trying to impress you with her bird knowledge. I think she secretly dreams of being part of your gang." Jack felt a pang of guilt. He knew he'd been mean about the girl. "This morning, when she heard the police suspected you, she came into the shop in a terrible state. It took me ages to get sense out of her. Eventually she admitted that she'd found my tin and brought it here." He looked at Twitch. "I'm guessing the police found it?"

Twitch nodded.

"Did you tell them that it was Pippa's?" Mr Bettany asked.

Twitch shook his head.

"No, he didn't," Iris exclaimed, "and I couldn't work out why!"

"I said it wasn't mine," Twitch said. "That should've been enough. They should've listened to me. Those eggs are older than I am. I figured the NWCU would tell Inspector Khan that. There's no way I could've collected them. They're not good evidence."

"But why didn't you tell the police where you got the tin?" Twitch's mum asked.

"Pippa's only nine, Mum," Twitch replied. "She was already frightened when she brought it to me. I knew they weren't hers. I wasn't going to dob her in and put her through that kind of questioning!" He looked at Mr Bettany. "I thought she was probably protecting you and I don't think you are the egg thief."

Iris Featherstone gave Twitch a proud smile. Tears

welled up in her eyes. "But you've been banned from Aves Wood, pet. You should've told them."

"Banned from Aves Wood?" Mr Bettany frowned.

"That officious jobsworth Gary Allen turned up at the police station," Iris sniffed. "He said Twitch wasn't allowed into the nature reserve until the trial was over, and if he's found guilty, he'll be banned for life."

"Wait. What?" Mr Bettany sat bolt upright. "They've charged you?" Twitch nodded. "I'll go to the station right this instant and explain about the tin of eggs. I cannot believe they would prosecute on such flimsy evidence. Those eggs are ancient! Surely they can see that!" His face was going purple. "Twitch, I am so sorry. I'm grateful that you protected Pippa, but I never dreamed you'd be arrested—"

"It won't do much good, Mr Bettany," Twitch interrupted him. "The tin is circumstantial evidence, proof that egg collecting is the kind of thing I like to do. They're using the broken swallow eggs I keep on the mantelpiece in my bedroom as more proof that I'm obsessed with oology. They are charging me because they have a witness who claims to have seen me up the top of the pike, near the nest, the night of the theft. Conveniently, the police found a box of freshly stolen eggs buried in our hide this morning."

"He's being set up," Jack declared angrily.

"Who is this witness?" Mr Bettany looked grave.

"I don't know." Twitch shrugged. "Whoever it is, they picked me out of a line-up today."

"It's the egg thief!" Jack told Mr Bettany. "They planted the eggs in the hide and tipped the police off."

"What can I do?" Mr Bettany asked. "I want to help. As your employer I can vouch for your good character. Please. I must be able to do something?"

"Actually, Mr Bettany," Jack said, "we do have a plan and I think you could be a great help indeed."

"Tell me what to do," Mr Bettany said, "and I'll do it."

27
CRACKING

After Mr Bettany left, Jack asked if he might stay the night and keep Twitch company. Iris readily agreed and called his parents.

"Now we can spend all night figuring this case out if we have to," Jack told Twitch.

"Let's go up on the roof to talk," Twitch suggested. "I don't want Mum to hear us, and I need to check on the pigeons."

"I sent Frazzle home this morning," Jack told him as they climbed upstairs.

He perched on the window ledge, watching, whilst Twitch opened up the loft and fussed around his birds. Frazzle was sitting in his nesting box. Twitch topped up his grain in the feeding bowl.

"Are you OK?" Jack asked.

"Dunno." Twitch gave him a weak smile. "When

I was being questioned today, about loving birds, the officers talked about it like it was a weird hobby. They called me 'odd' and seemed to think it was the kind of thing shady people might do." His voice was raw and emotional. "They described my love for birds as an 'unhealthy obsession' and spoke to me in a horrid way. They said keeping pigeons in a wardrobe wasn't normal." He shook his head. "Why isn't it normal to love birds?"

"It is," Jack assured him.

"I thought people round here understood who I was," Twitch said, shutting up the coop. "Now…" He shrugged.

"You mustn't take what happened at the police station to heart," Jack said, trying to cheer up his friend. "It's a tactic they use, to get people to confess. There'll be one good cop who's nice and offers you a drink, and one bad cop who calls you names. Between them they try to get to the truth. I've seen it in cop movies and detective shows." He patted Twitch's arm. "They're just doing their job."

"I guess," Twitch said, scratching at a fleck of mud on his trousers. "They found my binoculars."

"That's great!"

"Except they're using them as evidence against me. Inspector Khan said that someone handed them in, claiming to have found them on Friday morning, at the base of the rocks, below the nest."

"What!" Jack couldn't believe what he was hearing. "But, that's not possible! I saw you with them at school on Friday."

"I know."

"But this is good. We can prove they're lying. Who do you think the witness is, the one who said they saw you up the pike?"

"Don't know." Twitch shrugged. "Although I do know it's a man because they accidentally referred to the witness as 'he'." He looked up and scanned the skies. After a long moment he sighed. "Last year the swallows had arrived by now. I hope they're all right."

"Twitch." Jack pulled out his notebook and sat down on the roof. "We need to concentrate. The thief was in our hide this morning. I think they saw their egg-blowing kit and panicked. That must've been when they planted the eggs and tipped off the police. They know we're on to them."

"The egg-blowing kit is gone?" Twitch sat down opposite Jack, suddenly focused. "I'm worried the thief saw the spoonbills."

"The birds have been mostly hidden behind the reeds on the south bank of the pond. I think they'll be all right. Listen, I wanted to narrow down our suspect list, because we know it's not Mr Bettany and Pippa, and I'm pretty sure it's not Phil Gordon or Henley Brandy."

"Why not Henley?"

"He's obsessed with fish and not interested in birds, kind of like Phil Gordon. He's allergic to eating eggs, thinks they're gross, and, well, he's nice."

"So who's left?"

"Chris Merriman didn't arrive until after the eggs were stolen." Jack crossed out the names. "That just leaves us with three suspects."

"It's Jed Butler," Twitch said with cold certainty.

"Constable Greenwood says Jed Butler is reformed, but I agree we can't rule him out." He drew a question mark beside his name. "Too many things point at him. There's that cut on his forehead, and the night you lost your binoculars you saw him in his car. He could've seen you drop them and handed them in to put you in the picture, lying about when and where he'd got them."

"That's exactly what he did do," Twitch said. "And the witness who picked me out of the line-up is a man. I'll bet it was him. Did I tell you Vernon was in the line-up? All the other boys were Junior Cadets."

"The last suspects on the list are Merle and Evelyn

Drake." Jack scratched his head as he looked at their names. "I wanted to ask you something."

"What?"

"You remember when you helped Evelyn Drake, after she saved Gilbert?" Twitch nodded. "That was just along from Aves Lock, wasn't it?" Twitch nodded again. "Did you actually see the fox that she says she clobbered with her stick?"

Twitch frowned as he thought back. "No, it had run off. Why?"

"You said she had a nasty scratch on her wrist."

"So? Jed Butler has a scratch on his head and Henley Brandy's knuckles are red raw."

"But you said Gilbert's nest was along that bit of canal?"

"You can't seriously think Mrs Drake is the egg thief?" Twitch almost laughed he found the idea so ridiculous.

"No, I'm trying to rule suspects out," Jack said. "And I can't rule out the Drakes yet. I saw Evelyn in the woods this morning, and Henley said she wouldn't let him try on her hat. I remembered you saying she snatched it when you tried to pick it up for her."

"So, she likes her hat! Neither of the Drakes fit the profile of the egg thief. They are too old to go climbing

245

big rocks at the tops of hills. They aren't loners, they're a married couple and … well … they're nice!"

Jack nodded; Twitch was right. "I'm just trying to do things properly, be a good detective."

"This thief doesn't care that he's set me up to pay for his crimes," Twitch said. "He's dangerous, quick-thinking and sly. I'm telling you, it's Jed Butler."

Jack had to admit it did look that way. The Drakes had been nothing but sweet, but there was something about Evelyn that was troubling him.

"I've got a lot riding on that fake nest," Twitch said, looking anxious. "Let's hope the sting works."

"It'll work," Jack said, to reassure himself as well as his friend. If Twitch was banned from Aves Wood and the hide was destroyed, it could be the end of the Twitchers for ever. He wasn't about to let that happen. "I know it will work; it has to."

28

BAITING THE HOOK

Jack checked his watch. It was 8 a.m. He and Twitch had seen to the birds, eaten breakfast and were waiting in Twitch's front room for the others to arrive.

"I see them," Twitch said, pointing out the window at Terry, Ozuru, Tara, Ava and Tippi marching up the road. "They look like they're on a mission." He went to open the front door.

All five Twitchers filed past him into the front room wearing expressions of grim determination.

"We've got to keep our voices down," Twitch said in a whisper as he closed the front-room door. "Mum is worried about me getting into more trouble. She's happy to drive us to see Mr Landrow and get the eggs, but then I've got to come home."

"You can't come with us?" Tara asked softly.

"Mum's doing the late shift at the care home today.

She'll go to work after lunch. I'll be able to sneak out then."

"Who's got Twitch's disguise?" Jack asked.

"Terry's brother's red tracksuit bottoms, a baggy blue T-shirt, a black puffer coat, and a Yankees cap," Ava said, holding up a carrier bag.

Ozuru opened his rucksack and took out a pair of brightly coloured trainers with bubble soles and a glasses case containing a pair of round silver-framed glasses. "These are very fashionable trainers and my old glasses."

Twitch stared at the outfit.

"I'm going to do your hair," Ava told him.

"My hair!" Twitch's hands flew to his fringe.

"It makes you stand out," Tara said. "Not many boys have shoulder-length hair."

"Relax. I'm not going to cut it," Ava told him. "Just pin it into a style so that, when you're wearing the cap, it will look short. It'll help you blend in."

"Oh, OK." Twitch took the carrier bag, putting the trainers and glasses into it. "We'll do that once Mum's at work. I'd better hide this."

"Ava, Tara and Tippi," Jack said, "you'll go with Twitch to get the fake eggs. When we're done here, me, Ozuru and Terry will go to the hide. We're going to install the fake nest in the tree on the east side of the pond and set up the traps. Aves Wood should be pretty empty today because it's the final day of the Canal Masters, but we'll need to be stealthy. We don't want anyone to see us with the nest; it would ruin the whole plan."

"We can row the nest across the pond in the boat," Ozuru suggested. "That way we won't have to carry it through the wood. Less chance of being seen."

"Good idea," Jack said.

"By the time you have it in position, we should be back with the eggs," Tara said.

"The police said I had to stay away from birding areas," Twitch said.

"People from Briddvale don't know me or Tippi," Ava said. "If you stick with us when you're in disguise, no one will suspect who you are."

"The police think they've caught the egg thief. They won't be in Aves Wood," Tara pointed out. "But we will need to be on the lookout for the committee members."

"Yesterday evening, while we were watching over the spoonbills," Terry said, "Ozuru cloaked the crow's nest with camouflage netting. If you hide up there, no one will be able to see you."

"Everything needs to be in place before five o'clock," Jack said, turning to Ozuru, "which is when the Canal Masters will finish and the winners will be announced."

Ozuru nodded.

"Mr Bettany told us that after the weighing and the announcement, everyone is going to the Sozzled Stork," Twitch said. "Kenneth Mulworthy has given them the back room to celebrate and toast the winners. Mr Bettany is going to go around the room telling everyone that he's seen a pair of spoonbills nesting in Aves Wood and give out the location of our dummy nest."

"Baiting the hook" – Ozuru waggled his eyebrows – "as people who fish say."

"Does everyone know what they have to do?" Jack asked, and they all nodded. "Good." He looked at Twitch. "See you in a bit."

Jack was half afraid he'd find the hide smashed up, or cordoned off with yellow tape, but it looked the same as ever. He guessed that now the police had charged Twitch, it was no longer of interest to them. As he came through the door, he paused to examine the disturbed earth where the small tin of eggs had been buried. Kneeling down, he spotted a spoon half hidden by the foliage at the bottom of the hide wall. He took out his phone, snapped a photo, then pulled a freezer bag from his back pocket, and gingerly guided the spoon in without touching it.

"What's that?" Terry asked.

"One of our spoons. My guess is the thief used it to dig the hole and hide the tin. It might have fingerprints on it."

"Good spot!" Ozuru said.

Jack took it into the cabin and gasped at the spectacular sight of a nest the size of a dog's bed sitting on the table. "Is that Tippi's nest?" he marvelled. "It's incredible!"

"Isn't it great?" Terry nodded. "She was at it all afternoon."

"It doesn't look like a human built it at all," Ozuru agreed.

"How are we going to get it to the other side of the pond without damaging it?" Jack wondered.

"Tara's already thought of that." Ozuru reached down and picked up two corners of an old curtain that had been placed underneath it like a tablecloth. "You take two corners and bring them up," he instructed. "Now we have a hammock to carry and protect the nest. It's not that heavy."

"Genius," Jack said.

"We need to sort out the boat before we move it," Terry said. "Also, someone should keep watch from the crow's nest, just in case the thief decides to come back. I don't mind doing that."

The three of them sprang into action. Terry shinned up the tree to keep watch. Ozuru and Jack carried the boat up to the hide. Taking a corner of the curtain in each hand, Jack brought the cloth up and the corners together at the same time as Ozuru. They carefully backed out of the cabin with the nest, then lowered it into the bottom of the boat, covering it with the ends of the curtain.

Ozuru dragged the boat into the water and Jack gave a whistle to signal to Terry that they were ready.

Stepping lightly into the craft, mindful of its delicate cargo, Jack and Ozuru each picked up an oar. Terry came haring out of the hide, down to the pond, and climbed into the prow of the dinghy. "There's no one about. If we can get across the pond quickly, we definitely won't have been seen."

Jack and Ozuru concentrated on rowing together, moving the craft swiftly and steadily through the water. Terry used his binoculars and called out directions, guiding them to the willow tree that Twitch had picked out for the sting operation.

As he rowed, Jack thought about all that had happened yesterday morning. His mind kept returning to the missing egg-blowing kit in the blue tartan pencil case. Was it Jed's? It didn't seem to fit somehow.

As they neared the willow tree, the tall rushes hid their boat from view. They had to move slowly, weaving and pushing through the water plants to get to shore. Terry rose to his feet, wobbling at the movement of the boat and, reaching up, grabbed a branch, pulling them hand over hand towards the bank.

Ozuru jumped out and tied up the dinghy. When they were ready, Jack picked up his two corners of curtain and they lifted the nest out of the boat.

"Phew! That was tense," Terry said, wiping his forehead with his sleeve.

"You didn't do anything!" Ozuru exclaimed.

"I mean, watching it was tense." Terry grinned.

"I'll climb into the tree," Jack said, stepping his left foot up onto a knot in the trunk and grabbing the branch above his head. He made his way to the spot where they were going to plant the nest, on the bones of the old one. Wrapping his legs around the trunk, he reached his arms down as far as he could. Ozuru held up his two corners of the curtain and Jack managed to grasp them between his fingertips. The two of them slowly lifted the nest into the tree, with Terry manoeuvring it through the branches from below. When it was resting on the old tangle of twigs, Jack let his curtain corners fall. Then, centimetre by centimetre, Ozuru tugged the curtain out from under the nest.

In his excitement to get to the ground and see the nest in position, Jack didn't look before he jumped. He landed in water up to his knees. Terry and Ozuru chuckled as he sloshed out of the bog onto firmer ground. "It's so hard to see where the ground ends and the water starts."

"The nest looks amazing," Ozuru said.

"Is it a bit too … neat?" Jack wondered.

"Yes." Terry pulled a carrier bag from his coat pocket. "Tippi said I was to tease some sticks out and she gave me this." He opened the bag. It contained moss, white feathers and dried seed heads.

Ozuru set about pulling at the edges of the nest, spreading the sticks wider so it looked like it had been built in the tree, while Jack and Terry tucked moss into cracks, scattered seed heads and placed the feathers in and around it.

"Beautiful." Jack dusted off his hands. "Now all we need are eggs."

When they got back to the hide, they took it in turns to keep watch from the crow's nest. Jack was pleased to note that, through his binoculars, he could clearly see the nest.

"The others are here!" he called out, spotting four familiar figures on the footpath. Hanging the crow's nest binoculars on their twig, he climbed down. "Wait till you see Twitch's disguise."

Twitch had adopted a swagger to go with his new clothes. The effect was disarming. His long hair was gone, revealing a scrawny neck. Ava had let some of his fringe stick out from under the brim of the cap. Ozuru's glasses and the hat hid the top of Twitch's face. The joggers and enormous T-shirt that stretched down almost to his knees made him look like a skater kid.

"Not even your mum would recognize you," Ozuru said, impressed.

"Tippi, your nest is amazing!" Jack said.

"We got it into the tree, no problem," Ozuru told her.

"I want to see it." Tippi clapped excitedly.

"I'll come," Twitch said. "We can put the eggs in it together."

"Be careful." Jack pointed to his wet shins.

"Show us the eggs," Terry said.

They crowded around as Twitch opened the cardboard box. Inside were three white eggs with caramel flecks about seven centimetres in length.

"Can I touch one?" Jack asked.

"They're not fragile," Twitch said, handing him one. "They're made of a plastic resin."

"They look so real!" Terry marvelled.

"Exactly," Twitch said with grim satisfaction. "All the better to catch an evil egg snatcher." He took the egg back from Jack. "Right, Tippi, let's go put them in your nest."

"Twitch…" Jack began, but Tippi held up her hand.

"We're not using his name," she informed him. "We're calling him James. If you use his name, it gives him away."

"Oh! Good point. Erm, James…"

Twitch grinned. "Yes, Jack."

"Thought you should know, you can see the dummy nest from our crow's nest. With your long-lens camera, you should be able to take pictures of it. If we can snap a picture of the thief in the act of stealing the eggs, the evidence will be undeniable."

"I'd like to go to the canal and see how Dad's getting on," Ozuru said.

"I'd like to keep an eye on our suspects," Jack said.

"I think at least one of us should be here at all times," Terry said. "You know, to keep watch. I don't mind volunteering."

"You're not avoiding Pam, are you?" Tara asked,

teasing him. "She said she was filming the competition results."

"No!" Terry's cheeks went pink.

"I'd forgotten about Pam and Clem," Jack said, his mind whirring. "Vernon's by the canal today too. I think it's time we called on the honorary Twitchers for tonight's mission."

"But Pam's my mortal enemy!" Terry protested.

"We need all the help we can get," Jack insisted. "If we fail tonight, the spoonbills lose their babies, Twitch is banned from Aves Wood, and our hide will be destroyed."

"You're going to have to bury the hatchet with Pam," Ozuru told Terry.

"Fine." Terry nodded, then muttered to himself, "I'll bury it in her camera."

29

THE SOZZLED STORK

Dressed all in black, Jack led Terry, Ava and Ozuru on their bikes up to the Sozzled Stork. The pub was an old country inn with whitewashed walls, a low ceiling of black beams, and a fire in the grate of the main bar. Terry took them through the garden and past a playset of swings to the back room, which was a modern rectangular extension sticking out of the rear of the old building. It had double-glazed windows and chairs arranged around the edge of the room. Keeping low, communicating only with sign language, the four of them lined up along the brick wall, below an open window.

Tara and Tippi had remained at the hide, to keep watch on the spoonbills and the fake nest in case the thief made a surprise appearance. Twitch had wanted to come to the Sozzled Stork too, but they had all insisted he stay at home, pointing out that he needed an alibi should they fail, get caught, or more eggs were stolen. If Twitch was seen in the woods, at night, it would convince anyone in doubt that he was guilty. He'd also be in double the trouble for disobeying the police. After a short, heated discussion, Twitch had agreed to go home and spend the evening playing backgammon with Amita. Jack promised to message him as soon as they had caught the thief.

Peeping up over the window ledge, Jack scanned the room. A table with bowls of crisps and peanuts stood beside the door. Canal Masters competitors were beginning to arrive, having taken their fishing gear home and got changed. Mr Bettany wandered in with a pint of beer. He scanned the windows, spotted Jack, and sauntered over to sit on the chair beside the open window. He lifted his pint, so that his mouth was obscured, and whispered, "The eagle has landed."

"What does that mean?" Jack hissed.

"Just a little joke."

"This is serious!"

Vernon Boon came into the room clutching a glass of orange juice. Jack had told him he was going undercover and that he had to go wherever Jed Butler went.

"Vernon looks nervous," Ava whispered.

"Harry." Chris Merriman came and sat beside Mr Bettany. "Well, we didn't win, but we had fun." He lifted his glass. "Cheers! Beryl Crocker's looking pretty tickled at coming first. She's a worthy winner."

"Have you heard the news?" Mr Bettany said enthusiastically. "A pair of spoonbills are nesting in Aves Wood pond! How about that, eh?"

"Spoonbills?" Chris looked perplexed by this sudden shift in the conversation.

"It's a white wader," Mr Bettany told him.

"Oh." Chris sounded nonplussed. "Like a goose?"

"Not quite. Now, let me tell you all about waders, they're fascinating birds," Mr Bettany said. "I'm an avid birder you see, and—"

"I'd love to hear about it later, but I need to have a quick word with Phil. He's pretty down about coming third…" Chris said, rising hurriedly.

Mr Bettany chuckled as Chris walked away. "Well, he's not our man," he said under his breath.

"Tell the Drakes about the spoonbill nest," Jack hissed. He was interested to see their reactions, particularly Evelyn's.

Jed Butler sloped into the room and helped himself to a handful of crisps.

"There's Jed Butler," Jack said. "Make sure he knows."

Mr Bettany raised his glass at Jed Butler, who nodded his head then went to sit on the other side of the room.

"Charming," Mr Bettany muttered.

"Harry," Evelyn Drake called out. "You're not sitting on your own?"

"Ah, Evelyn, you must be glad the fishing is over," Mr Bettany greeted Mrs Drake as she came towards him.

"To be honest," she said, sighing as she sat down, "I'll be glad to get home to my garden. Merle's never happier than when he's fishing, but there are only so many walks I can go on before my knees start complaining. Age is a terrible affliction."

"Oh, I hear you. I envy Merle's passion. Fishing is a wonderful pursuit. Just wish I was better at it." Mr Bettany chuckled. "Now, if there were birdwatching competitions, I'm certain I could win one of those."

"Ah, you like birds, do you?"

"That I do." Mr Bettany nodded. "Do you know, there's a pair of spoonbills nesting on the east side of the pond in Aves Wood? In a willow tree hanging over the water. I'm going to take a look at them tomorrow, now that the Canal Masters is over. They're rare birds to find in these parts."

"A what did you call them?"

"Spoonbill."

"Don't tell me, they have a beak shaped like a spoon?"

"They do." Mr Bettany grinned, and Mrs Drake chuckled.

"I don't know who was put in charge of naming all the creatures, but at times I think they ran out of ideas. I'm more of a wildflower fan myself. I like the birds, but I can only identify the common ones. I can't say that I've ever seen a spoonbill."

"Oh, they're lovely birds."

"You should talk to young Jed Butler about birds. He loves them." She nodded towards the sullen shaven-headed figure who was sitting awkwardly beside Vernon Boon. Neither of them was talking.

"He does?" Mr Bettany asked.

"Oh, yes, it's all he's been talking about back at the campsite. I'm sure he'd be thrilled to hear there are spoonbeaks here if they're rare."

"Spoonbills," Mr Bettany corrected her, and Jack's suspicion that she might be the thief crumbled.

"What did I say?"

"Spoonbeaks."

"Spoonbill, spoonbeak, it's all the same to me." She made a high noise and waved to Beryl Crocker. "Will you excuse me? I must ask Beryl what her secret is. Merle is sure she must have a secret bait recipe to have caught the quantity of fish she did today. I told him there is no recipe for a woman's intuition." And with a delighted chuckle, she tottered off.

"She didn't seem that interested either," Mr Bettany whispered.

"Go and talk to Jed Butler," Jack hissed. "And tell him exactly where the spoonbill nest is."

Mr Bettany got up, approaching Jed and Vernon in a roundabout way, chatting briefly to Phil Gordon, saying something to Beryl Crocker. Jack watched eagerly as finally Mr Bettany approached Jed. He focused on Jed's lips, reading every word exchanged between the two men.

"What's he saying?" Terry whispered.

"Not much," Jack grumbled. "It's mostly grunts, nods and, 'Oh really?'. That sort of thing. Jed Butler is a hard man to read." He paused. "Oh, great."

"What?" Ava asked.

"Mr Bettany told Jed about the spoonbill nest. His reply was a shrug, then he said he needed to go to the loo!" Jack sighed; he'd hoped someone would react to the news in a revealing way.

"So nobody is interested in the spoonbills," Terry said. "What does that mean? Have we got the wrong suspects?"

"I don't know," Jack replied, trying to ignore the whispering doubts in his head. He had been so certain it had to be Evelyn Drake or Jed Butler. The thought that the sting might not work, and Twitch would get convicted of stealing eggs, was making him sick with nerves.

"Mr Bettany's talking to Merle Drake," Ava said.

Jack watched him tell Merle about the spoonbills. The man didn't look anything other than politely interested. It wasn't the reaction Jack had been hoping for.

A tinkling noise stopped all conversation.

Dr Sawa was standing in the middle of the room hitting his wine glass with a teaspoon.

"What's Dad doing?" Ozuru whispered.

"Ladies and gentlemen, may I have your attention? I have a little announcement." The room fell silent. "I have enjoyed your company this week. It has been an honour to fish with you all. I think everyone in this room knows that I wouldn't have had such a fine catch on Monday if Henley's bait hadn't been washed down to my peg." He smiled at the eccentric fisherman. "Today, Henley came second, proving that the fish of Briddvale really do like Mozart." There was a burst of appreciative laughter and Henley blushed with pleasure. "I don't wish to qualify for the next round of the Canal Masters at his expense. Therefore, if the judges will allow it, I would like to transfer my catch on Monday to Henley, forfeiting my place in the next round of the competition."

There was much murmuring at this news.

Henley looked stunned.

"Now, hang on a minute!" Phil Gordon stood up. "If you forfeit your position, then I come second overall."

"If I'm not allowed to transfer my catch to Henley, then I won't forfeit my position," Dr Sawa replied calmly and firmly.

"Well, now. This is most irregular," the head judge said, standing up. "I will need to consult with my fellow judges." And they went into the corner to confer.

Phil Gordon glowered, Henley looked bemused, and Dr Sawa smiled.

"What did your dad do that for?" Terry asked Ozuru.

"The next round of the competition is on a canal four hours' drive away," Ozuru said. "Dad's got his surgery. He won't be able to go. He knows he didn't deserve to win. He's not the best fisherman. He must've thought this was the honourable thing to do."

"I think it's nice," Ava said.

"We've made our decision." The head judge came to stand in the middle of the room. "We will adjust our table of winners. Beryl is the outright winner, as before." There was a cheer. "We've decided that second place" – everyone held their breath – "will be awarded jointly to Henley Brandy and Phil Gordon. All three contestants will be going through to the next round."

"Yes!" Phil Gordon punched the air, his face bright red.

Henley Brandy looked flabbergasted and stared open-mouthed at Beryl as she congratulated him heartily.

"Where is he?" Jack hissed.

"Who?" Ava asked urgently.

"Jed Butler." Jack scanned and rescanned the room.

"Quick! Jed's done a runner," said a voice behind them. Jack spun around to see Vernon standing on the path. "He said he was going to the loo, but I've checked the toilet. He's not there."

"He's fallen for the sting!" Ava exclaimed in amazement.

"He's taken the bait," Ozuru said.

Jack looked back through the window at Mr and Mrs Drake, who were chatting happily with Beryl Crocker. "Right," he said, turning away. "We have to get to the nest before Jed Butler does!"

30
SPRUNG!

Jack darted away from the window, crouching low as he ran. The others followed. The four of them grabbed their bikes, wheeling them out onto the road.

"Wait for me." Vernon pounded after them.

"Terry and Ozuru, you go to the campsite," Jack said. "My guess is that Jed Butler will go back there to get his egger equipment. When he leaves to go to Aves Wood, have a snoop around his tent. If you find anything that looks like evidence, like a collection of eggs, take photographs and then go to the police and report it. Remember to wear your gloves. We don't want your fingerprints all over everything."

"Er, that's not legal," Vernon said, climbing onto his bike. "It's breaking and entering."

"It's a tent. There's no lock. Nothing is being broken," Jack snapped.

"What if someone sees us?" Terry asked.

"Who is going to see you? Everyone is here." Jack waved his hand at the pub. "And, you know, try not to get caught! We're doing this to clear Twitch's name, remember?"

"Right. OK." Terry nodded as he and Ozuru cycled away slowly up the hill.

"I've sent a message to Tara," Ava told him.

"Now we spring our trap and catch Jed Butler red-handed," Jack said, a thrill of anticipation making him shiver as he sailed down the hill on his bike.

"I can't wait to see the look on his face when he realizes he's been tricked," Ava said. She was riding Twitch's bike beside him. "That'll teach him for framing Twitch."

When they reached Aves Wood, they hid their bikes in the bracken, turned on their head torches and hurried along the path. It was a clear, cold night and Jack glimpsed pin-prick stars through the canopy of trees.

"There's the shopping trolley tree," Ava said.

"Where are they?" Jack hissed, looking about for Tara and Tippi.

"Rats! We forgot there's no signal." Ava grabbed her head torch, held it up high and waved it madly. "If they are keeping watch, they should see this and come."

Sure enough, three minutes later they heard the two girls running through the trees.

"Hi," Tara greeted them breathlessly as she and Tippi appeared, dressed in black. She looked at Jack. "Did it work?"

"Jed Butler took the bait." Jack nodded.

"He did a runner," Vernon told her.

"Twitch was right!" Tara exclaimed in a whisper.

"Head torches off everyone," Ava said. "Ground torches on."

They did as she said, pulling lipstick-sized torches from their pockets. When they got to the part of the path where the hidden trail went to the willow tree, Jack called out in a low voice, "Pam? Clem?"

"You took your time," said Pam's sharp voice. There was a rustle and two pale faces appeared in the darkness. Pam and Clem emerged from the trail entrance. They too were dressed all in black. Pam had tucked her hair into a beanie.

"Good, you're here," Jack said. "Jed Butler left the party at the Sozzled Stork as soon as he heard about the spoonbills. He could be here any minute."

"What's the plan?" Clem asked.

"Along this path, there's a willow tree with a fake nest in it," Ava said.

"Tara and I built it," Tippi told Pam.

"Where's the real one?" Pam asked.

"On the south bank of the pond," Jack replied. "Our one has three fake spoonbill eggs in it. They are the bait for our trap." He grinned. "We'll all hide around the tree. When Jed Butler comes for the eggs, we watch and stay silent. You film him stealing them."

"There's a bit of a problem with that," Clem said. "It's dark. This camera's not very good at night." He held up his phone.

"Get what you can," Ava said.

"I've got a strong torch. When you give the signal, I can shine it on the thief," Pam said, holding up a large black light. "Then the camera will be able to catch him with the eggs in his hands."

"Then what happens?" Clem said.

"Vernon's going to make a citizen's arrest." Jack felt a surge of excitement as he said this.

"I brought handcuffs," Vernon said, pulling them out of his pocket.

"Are they real?" Clem asked.

"No, they're toy ones, but he won't know that."

"What if he doesn't want to come with us?" Pam asked. "He looks pretty strong."

"He'll have to come," Jack said, "because you will

have streamed the whole thing on the Internet. There'll be no point in him running away."

"Um, we can't do that," Clem said. "There's no phone or Internet signal in Aves Wood."

"Oh yeah!" Jack's stomach lurched. How had he forgotten that? And Pam was right. Jed Butler was very strong.

"What if he tries to do a runner?" Vernon asked him. "I am fast, and quite strong, but you know…" He looked nervous. "He's a grown-up."

"We'll call the police," Jack said.

"How are we going to do that, Einstein" – Pam's hands went to her hips – "when there's no signal?"

"I know," Tara said. "Tippi and I will hide opposite the entrance to the path. As soon as Jed Butler passes us, we'll sneak out to Crowther Bridge. I can call the police from there."

"Great." Jack felt relieved. "Yes. And if Jed struggles or tries to run, Ava, me and Clem will help. If four of us pin him down, he won't be able to get away."

"Unless he has a weapon," Vernon pointed out.

There was a horrible silence.

"If … er … he has a weapon…" Jack's throat had become dry. He hadn't thought this through as thoroughly as he ought to. His heartbeat picked up speed. "Then we get our evidence and we get out of here. Leave Jed Butler to the police."

"Where's Terry?" Pam asked.

"Gathering evidence," Ava replied.

"Is he coming later?"

"Now is not the time for pranks, Pam," Jack told her.

"This is serious," Tara said. "If we don't catch Jed Butler and prove Twitch isn't a thief, his life could be ruined."

"I wasn't going to!" Pam huffed.

"Where is Twitch?" Clem asked. "I thought he'd want to be here."

"He can't, police orders," Jack said. "Now, listen, we've laid down lots of twigs here, at the beginning of the path, so that we'll hear them snap as Jed comes this way."

"How can you be sure he'll come tonight?" Pam asked.

"Because the Canal Masters heat is over," Jack replied. "The competitors will be leaving tomorrow. This is his only chance to steal the eggs."

"But, you don't know that he's leaving, do you?" Pam narrowed her eyes.

Jack opened his mouth, then realized Pam was right. He'd assumed all the competitors would leave once the Canal Masters heat was over, because of what Ozuru had said, but he didn't *know* it. What if Jed didn't come?

He suppressed his sudden feeling of panic. No. The man had disappeared as soon as he'd heard about the spoonbills. He must be on his way here. Jack tried to calm his pattering pulse. Now wasn't the time for doubts. "He's coming," he assured her, "and we can't afford to muck this up. If we fail, Twitch will never be able to come to Aves Wood and our hide will be destroyed."

"Doesn't sound that bad," Pam muttered.

Ava gave her a death stare. "Jed will keep stealing eggs and murdering baby birds!"

"We shouldn't be standing around talking," Tara chastised them. "We should be getting into position."

The group dispersed. Tara and Tippi retreated into the bracken opposite the path. Everyone else followed Jack along the narrow marshy animal track between the bulrushes.

"Urgh, this place is gross," Pam whispered as her boot sank into the boggy ground.

Jack stopped when the willow tree was about three metres away. He pointed left. "Twitch cleared a space for you and Clem to hide in those rushes. There are two tree stumps for you to sit on. You should be able to see the nest clearly."

"That's the nest." Ava gestured to the dark shape on the low branch stretched over the edge of the pond.

"Don't walk along this path straight towards it," Jack said. "We've covered the ground with mulch so it looks like a path, but it's a trap. If you go that way, you'll be dumped into water up to your middle."

"Nice!" Pam looked impressed.

"Vernon, you'll be here." Jack pulled apart the wall of bulrushes to their right. Behind it was another tree stump. "Jed will walk right past you, so you need to be super silent. There's a rope tied to that tree and fed along the ground." He pointed to the end. "If he runs, and comes back this way, you can lift it to trip him, or use it to tie him up."

"Cool." Vernon nodded, stepping through the rushes and sitting down on the stump.

"Jack and I will be hiding beyond the tree," Ava said, "in case he approaches from another way."

"Which he won't," Jack said. "Because there is no other easy way to get to this tree."

"Got it," Pam said. "We won't reveal ourselves until you do."

"After Ava and I jump out, Vernon, you'll block his exit. You can read him his rights and arrest him." Their eyes sparkled in the darkness as they looked at each other. They were all nervous. "Let's get into position."

Jack found it very difficult to sit still on his tree

stump. What if Jed didn't come? How long should they wait? What if he did come, but had a weapon? Why hadn't he thought of that? He glanced at Ava, who had her arms wrapped around herself to ward off the cold and was staring fixedly at the dummy nest. The night air was biting, and he worried that the pale plumes of mist they exhaled might give them away. Just as he was beginning to despair, Jack heard the cracking sound of feet snapping twigs and the swish of moving foliage.

Ava's hand grabbed his knee and he almost cried out in alarm.

They exchanged a wide-eyed glance, suddenly sitting straight-backed, all thoughts of the cold gone.

Leaning forward, peering in the direction of the sound of reeds whipping against trouser legs, Jack heard a low mutter and laboured breathing. Then came the dancing light of a torch. It was pointing down at the ground. He saw walking boots. He stiffened. There were *two* pairs of walking boots coming along the path!

Jack's mind spun. They'd only planned to catch one thief!

"I see it," came a man's voice. "It's here!"

A second torch was switched on.

Standing on the trail, two steps from the water trap, were Merle and Evelyn Drake!

31

HUMPTY DUMPTY

Jack's heart was so loud he felt like it was beating between his ears.

The Drakes! Ava mouthed at him, looking alarmed.

Everything fell into place in Jack's head. He saw Evelyn Drake's shocked expression when he'd exploded out of the ferns yesterday morning. It had been him who had given away the location of the hide. All she'd had to do was follow the smell of fried bacon to find it. When she did, she must've seen her egg-blowing kit on the crime wall, grabbed Tara's Tupperware and planted the eggs – which means she'd had them on her! And the man who'd identified Twitch was Merle, not Jed at all! Pippa had said she saw an old man up the pike. It must've been him! He realized the reason the case had tied him in knots was because there were two thieves working together and he'd been looking for one!

"What do we do?" Ava signed.

"Same as before," he signed back.

"Aaaarrrgghhh!" Merle yelled as he sank up to his waist in water. His torch light blinked out.

Jack felt a smirk of satisfaction creep across his face. He hoped Pam was filming this.

"Shh!" Evelyn hissed. "Someone could hear you!"

"You shh!" he barked. "I've slipped into the ruddy pond! It's freezing! I knew this was a bad idea."

Evelyn tested the ground in front of her with her walking stick. She inched towards the nest, avoiding the trap.

"Help me out, Evelyn," Merle said, wading towards her. "I've lost my torch. I can't see a thing."

Evelyn exhaled a sigh of exasperation. "The ground is firm here. Take my hand." She reached out to him, leaning back as she hauled Merle free from the bog hole. He clambered out, covered in pond slime, and gave himself a shake.

Jack's smile faded. The pair weren't moving like they did during the day. He'd only ever seen Merle sitting in a chair and Evelyn leaning on her stick, but they moved with a strength and surety that surprised him.

"I see the nest," Evelyn said gleefully, leaping lightly onto the roots of the tree.

"The tougher the trail, the greater the prize, eh?" Merle moved after her.

"Precisely, my darling." She leaned back and kissed him. "There's nothing more thrilling than a midnight heist."

A break in the clouds allowed the moon's reflected beams to shine a dim light on the pair. Evelyn was wearing her hat and Merle had his arms around her. Jack realized with a start that he'd resigned them to "elderly" as soon as Mr Drake had said he was retired. He'd assumed they were the same age as Mr Bettany, but, looking at them now, he guessed they were in their forties. Had they been putting on an act? He saw the roots of Mr Drake's grey hair were dark. It was dyed!

"Ho, ho, what beauties." Merle rubbed his hands together as he glimpsed the three white ovals in their bed. "A fine addition to our collection."

"I'll climb up," Evelyn said. "You keep watch."

"No one is going to be out here at this time of night," Merle scoffed.

Jack was astonished to see that Evelyn Drake was as good at climbing as Ava. She moved up the tree and into the branches like a gymnast, then disappeared from view. Jack switched to looking intently at the nest and glimpsed the silhouette of a hand blotting out the pale glowing sphere of an egg. He cursed silently that he couldn't quite see what she was doing. *"I think she has the eggs,"* he signed to Ava.

Ava shot up and stepped through the bulrushes. "Stop right there!" she cried.

Vernon appeared on the path like a ghostly apparition. "Halt in the name of the law."

"What the—" Merle looked around as a bright light was shone on him. He raised a gloved hand to shield his eyes.

To Jack's surprise, Evelyn Drake emerged from behind the willow tree, coming to stand beside her husband. When had she climbed down?

"Ha haaaaa!" Pamela cried, emerging from the bulrushes with her microphone. "You're busted!"

Jack stumbled forward to stand beside Ava.

"We've caught you red-handed, you evil egg snatchers!" Pamela cried.

"Mr and Mrs Drake, I'm arresting you on suspicion of egg theft." Vernon turned on his head torch. "You do not have to say anything. But, it may harm your defence if you do not mention when questioned something which you later rely on in court. Anything you do say may be given in evidence." He smiled at Jack. "I've always wanted to say that."

"Don't worry, dear," Evelyn muttered to Merle. "It's just those children who think they're detectives."

"I see. Well," Merle said, stepping forward, "you've had your fun, now buzz off."

"Mr and Mrs Drake, I'm afraid I'm going to have to request that you both accompany me to the police station to answer a few questions," Vernon said.

"Are you now?" Merle sounded annoyed. "And what is this all about, may I ask?"

"You've been caught stealing eggs from a spoonbill nest," Pam declared dramatically. She turned to look at the camera. "This is Pamela Hardacre, undercover!"

"I beg your pardon?" Evelyn said, almost apologetically. "I'm sorry, little girl, but we haven't taken eggs from a nest." She held out her hands, which were empty, and looked disdainfully at Pam. "Is this for a school project?"

"You have. They're in your pockets," Pam said, sounding less sure of herself. "But we tricked you, because the real spoonbill nest is on the south bank of the pond."

Jack winced as she said this. The location of the nest was meant to be kept secret.

"Search me if you like," Evelyn said, turning out her coat pockets. "You won't find any eggs. I would never do such a heartless thing as to steal from a bird!" She smiled, then looked up at her hat. "Oh! In case you were wondering…" She lifted the hat off, showing them it was empty, before placing it back on her head.

"Come on," Merle waved Vernon forward and stood with his legs apart, stretching out his arms. "I suppose you want to search me, do you?"

Vernon shuffled forward and awkwardly patted him down. He turned around and looked at Jack. "Er. He doesn't seem to have anything in his pockets."

Ava strode past Evelyn and climbed the tree. "The nest is empty."

"We saw you take the eggs," Jack said to Evelyn. "You must've hidden them in the reeds or, or … dropped them in the water."

"Did you hear anything drop into the water?" Merle asked innocently.

Jack had to shake his head. He hadn't.

"Actually, I couldn't see the nest from where I was sitting," Vernon admitted.

"Me neither," Pam said, and Clem shook his head.

"Did you see the Drakes take the eggs, Jack?" Vernon asked.

"I didn't have a clear view, but I saw the eggs in the nest, and then Mrs Drake climbed the tree. I saw the shadow of a hand … and Mr Drake said they were beauties."

"I saw the same as you," Ava said quietly.

"You're mistaken, lad, I didn't say anything about eggs. I was referring to the stars. They are beautiful, and I'm sorry but I haven't seen any eggs."

"Nor I," Evelyn Drake agreed.

"But you said it was a fine night for a midnight heist, and … and … you said you were going to add them to your collection," spluttered Jack.

"I'm afraid you misheard me," Evelyn said with a flinty smile. "I said it was a fine night for a midnight feast, and what my darling husband meant about our collection, is that we would be adding this experience to our collection of wonderful nights together."

Jack was shocked by these lies, told so confidently.

"Can I ask what you and your husband are doing out in Aves Wood at this time of night?" Vernon asked, with the adopted tones of a policeman.

"Tonight is our last night in Briddvale," Evelyn replied, putting her hand on Merle's arm. "We thought we'd take a romantic walk, by moonlight, around the pond, and find a lovely tree to climb, where we could look over the water and have a midnight feast together. It's a little tradition of ours."

"Er. Right, then. Um." Vernon stepped back from the path. "Um, please accept my apologies. You are free to go."

"What?!" Jack exclaimed as the Drakes walked away from the tree. "No! Wait!"

"This was fun," Evelyn said as they walked away, "but I'm afraid we will have to report you. Impersonating a police officer is a crime, you know."

"He's a Police Cadet!" Jack spat, lurching forward, propelled by anger. He tripped on a willow tree root, sidestepped to recover his balance and, gasping in shock, suddenly found himself waist-deep in pond water. Clem turned the spotlight and camera on him.

"Don't let them get away," Jack shouted at Vernon. "The nest is empty! They must have the eggs!"

Vernon was shaking his head. "There's nothing we can do, Jack. None of us saw what she did with the eggs, and without them, or two strong witnesses, it's our word against theirs. They're grown-ups." He shrugged. "I think we're going to be in big trouble over this. I hope they don't kick me out of Junior Cadets."

"But the Drakes are the egg thieves!" Jack cried, his heart sinking as he pictured the look on Twitch's face when he told him what had happened. The sting had been such a brilliant plan and he had mucked it up.

"It wasn't a complete waste of time," Pam said, as Ava helped Jack out of the water trap. "The camera picked up next to nothing in the dark, but we've got Jack falling in the water. We can add that to the Pranks Playlist."

Vernon, Pam and Clem started making their way along the track, going slowly so as not to catch up with the Drakes.

Ava looked at Jack. "What do we do now?"

32

THE CALL OF THE NIGHTJAR

A whirlwind of worries hit Jack. He'd sent Terry and Ozuru to search Jed Butler's tent! And told Tara and Tippi to call the police the moment the egg thief set foot on the trail. Were they coming? He listened for the sound of sirens. Somehow, right in front of him, Evelyn Drake had managed to steal three fake spoonbill eggs. It had been a perfectly good plan and he'd totally messed up everything! Because of him, Twitch would be labelled a thief for ever. The schemes they'd hatched to spend the summer in the hide, watching birds, became ashes in his mind. The hide would be bulldozed. Twitch would be banned. The Twitchers would be finished and the Drakes would keep stealing eggs. Jack felt like crying. Only Ava's cool, angry presence stopped him.

"What did she do with those eggs?" Ava was studying the ground, moving her torch in sweeping motions.

"We both saw her hand dart out and take them." She pointed her torch at the tree. "The nest is empty – they've gone – so where did she put them? They didn't go in the water; we would've heard a splash."

"Vernon searched her," Jack said, feeling like he was sinking into the marsh as his freezing wet trousers clung to his legs.

"Where did she put them?" Ava muttered to herself. "She didn't have a bag."

"I don't know," Jack said despairingly.

"Not giving up, are you, Cappleman?" Ava's mocking tone and use of his surname worked like a metaphorical slap around the face.

"No." Jack pulled himself up.

"Good. Then work out what she did with the eggs."

"I thought she'd hidden them in her hat, until she lifted it off her head and showed us the inside."

"Me too," Ava agreed. "Odd that she did that, though."

"Shh!" Jack suddenly became aware of a high alien bird call. He stopped still. "Listen! It's a nightjar!"

"So?"

"So, nightjars only call at dawn or at dusk." Jack gave Ava a meaningful look. "They do not call in the middle of the night."

"*So?*" Ava repeated.

"The nightjar is Twitch's spark bird," Jack said, looking out across the still, dark surface of the pond. Another eerie call spurred him into a run. "He's here. Come on."

"Twitch?" Jack whispered as he and Ava approached the hide. "Are you there?"

"Shh," a shadow hissed.

Ava grabbed his hand and Jack nearly jumped out of his skin. They both heard Tippi giggle.

"Tippi," Ava whispered, seeing her little sister's head peeping out the cabin window. "What are you doing here? I thought you were with Tara."

"Come inside." Tippi waved them to the door.

The tepee entrance was dark but there was a dim light in the cabin. Spare strips of the camp tarpaulin had been hung over the window and the door.

Tara and Twitch were sitting at the table, having a whispered conversation.

"Twitch!" Jack said. "What are you doing here?" He saw that his friend had on black waders over his camos, a black fleece and a black beanie. He'd come prepared for action.

"You didn't really think I was going to stay at home

playing backgammon with Amita?" Twitch said. "She's a terrible cheat and always wins."

"But … how—"

"Listen, I saw everything," Twitch cut him off. "From up in the crow's nest. I saw the Drakes come into the wood by the east gate. Their car is parked up on the Briddvale Road. I think they're planning to grab those spoonbill eggs and hightail it out of here."

"What!"

"I was coming to help you catch them when I met Tara and Tippi by the path."

"I tried…" Jack felt a burning wave of shame wash over him.

"No, I should've listened to you," Twitch said. "Jack, you wanted to investigate the Drakes, but I was so sure it was Jed Butler."

"We called the police, Jack," Tara said. "I wasn't sure if I should when I saw who the thieves were, but I did it anyway." She bit her lip, looking worried that she'd done the wrong thing.

"Then Pam opened her big mouth," Twitch said, pulling a thick coil of rope over his head so that it hung diagonally across his chest, "and told the Drakes the nest was a fake and the real one was on the south bank. As soon as I heard that, we raced back here."

"How could you hear us?" Jack asked, wrapping his arms around himself as he shivered. His wet legs felt like icicles.

"Parabolic microphone." Twitch grinned. "I had it with me. Tippi watched the Drakes go back to their car from the crow's nest. It's parked where Henley's moped was the other day."

"Mr Drake changed into dry clothes. Then they packed a bag," Tippi said. "I couldn't see what went in it."

"Tara rowed out into the pond with my phone to play the nightjar call," Twitch said. "I hoped you'd hear it."

"You couldn't have known that we would," Ava said.

"There was a good chance. When sound travels over water, it's louder, and Jack knows the call," Twitch said, picking up a large torch. He clicked it once and it shone red; he clicked it twice and it shone white. He handed the torch to Ava. "And, nightjars don't call at this time of night."

Jack felt a stab of pride that he'd known this and recognized the signal for what it was. "Do you have a plan?"

"Yes. We do the only thing that's important," Twitch replied. "We protect those spoonbills." He turned to

Tara and Tippi. "Me, Jack and Ava are going to cross the pond in the boat. You two, hide near Crowther Bridge. When the Drakes come back into Aves Wood, go find their car and take pictures of what can be seen through the windows. You'll need a torch." Tippi held up hers. "If the police do come, get them to search the car. The peregrine falcon eggs must be in there somewhere."

The two girls nodded.

"We can't let the Drakes leave Briddvale with those eggs."

"Got it," Tara said.

"I don't suppose anyone's got spare trousers I could borrow?" Jack pointed to his sodden legs. "I'm freezing."

"Terry's rucksack is in the triangle room," Tara said. "You could look in there."

"Be quick," Twitch said. "We need to go."

Jack emptied the contents of Terry's rucksack out and found Ava's purple joggers. He wriggled out of his wet trousers, drying his goose-pimply legs with a T-shirt, and pulled Ava's trousers on. Terry was right, they were soft and warm. He immediately felt better and put on a pair of Terry's threadbare socks.

"Come on," Twitch called, marching to the boat. "We have to get to the spoonbill nest before the Drakes do."

Ava, Jack and Twitch boarded the dinghy.

"Good luck," Tara whispered, as Tippi blew them kisses.

Twitch sat in the prow of the boat as Ava and Jack rowed.

"When I heard the Drakes coming into Aves Wood," Twitch whispered, "I felt terrible. Jack, I stopped you from solving the case. You suspected them, but I wouldn't listen." He shook his head. "You were right. Poor Gilbert must've been protecting his nest from Evelyn. She whacked him with that stick of hers and broke his wing. There was no fox."

"It's not your fault," Jack said. "I should've trusted my gut."

"From now on, I'll do the bird protecting and let you do the detecting."

"Sounds good." Jack smiled. "The man Pippa saw on the pike, I think it was…"

"Merle." Twitch nodded.

"Have you noticed he always wears gloves?" Jack said. "I'll bet if he takes them off, we'll see his hands are covered in talon scratches."

"I hope so," Ava said through gritted teeth.

"Evelyn and Merle have been acting older than they really are," Jack said. "His hair is dyed grey, and she doesn't need that stick. She climbed the tree almost as well as Ava."

"How did they find out about our hide?" Ava said.

"That's my fault," Twitch and Jack said at the same time.

"I told Evelyn we had a hide," Twitch admitted.

"I came pelting out of the ferns by the shopping trolley tree and nearly knocked her over," Jack said. "I might as well have pointed and showed her the way." He pictured her digging up the ground in the hide with the spoon. "She's a nasty piece of work."

"Merle fishes whilst Evelyn hunts for nests, and then they go out together under the cover of darkness and collect the eggs." Ava shuddered. "That's so gross."

"Wait, Twitch. You were watching us through your camera? Did you see Evelyn take the fake eggs?"

"Yes."

"Do you know where she hid them?"

In the moonlight, Jack saw the white of Twitch's teeth as he smiled. "Yes, I did, and I took pictures."

33

EGGSPOSED!

Twitch held up his hands as their boat reached the middle of the pond. "We need to go in close to the shore so I can stand up in the water, but we should switch to signing. We don't want to startle birds or let the Drakes know we're here. You two, stay in the boat," he instructed in a low whisper. "Otherwise you'll end up getting wet. The ground is treacherous along the shore." He turned to Ava. "If you spot the Drakes, flash the red beam to alert me. Then switch off the torch."

"What about me?" Jack said. "I want to come with you."

Twitch looked down at his waders and then pointedly at Jack's purple joggers.

"You are not going for a swim in my trousers," Ava said.

"I brought the sack of fat balls." Twitch pointed at

the shapeless lump at the bottom of the boat. "Fire them at anyone who goes near that nest."

"Got it." Jack nodded. "What are you going to do?"

"I'm going to make sure the Drakes can't get near those birds." Twitch patted the coil of rope around his body. Looking over the prow, he tried to assess the depth of the water. "I'll get out over there." He pointed to a patch of bulrushes and they steered the boat silently towards it.

Careful not to rock the boat, Twitch stepped first one leg, then the other, over the side. Concentrating on finding the bottom of the pond with his feet, he swallowed a gasp as the cold water rose right up to his hips.

"*You OK?*" Jack signed and Twitch nodded.

Taking one step at a time, Twitch moved through the water, heading towards the bank a good distance from the spoonbill nest. The pulse in his ears seemed to mark the seconds ticking by. There was no sight or sound of the Drakes yet. He needed to get into position before they arrived.

Reaching the bank, he glanced over his shoulder. Jack and Ava were huddled together in the boat, both watching him intently, Ava hugging the torch. Twitch turned his concentration to clambering through the reeds and out of the water. His hands were freezing. He wished he'd thought to wear gloves.

How far away were the Drakes now? he wondered, as he picked his way onto firmer ground. He needed to hurry. When he'd studied his photos of the land around the nest, he'd picked out a tree in a good position that he thought was climbable, but, in the dark, he wasn't sure which tree it was. Taking a guess, he scrambled up into the branches of an old elm tree, which turned out to be tricky, and slippery, wearing wet waders. All he could hear was the sound of his own heavy breathing as he found a sturdy branch and took off the two ropes he'd brought, looping both around the trunk and then over the bough. Scrambling back down the tree, he searched for a large piece of deadwood. He needed something heavy. He saw a felled tree, lying on its side, rotting. He kicked at it and the trunk crumbled. Kneeling down, he prised it apart, tearing off a large hunk of log, disrupting a scurry-load of black beetles. Tucking the log into his waders, he scaled the elm and tied it to the end of one of the ropes. Now, he had to wait.

The shushing sound of rustling leaves, followed by the crack of stems and sticks snapping, made him turn his head. He saw Ava's red signal. Then all was dark. *They were coming!*

"What was that?" Merle's gruff voice said.

"What?" Evelyn answered.

"I saw a red flash."

"I didn't see anything."

"Over the water."

"Probably a car headlight," Evelyn said, dismissing it.

The Drakes weren't cautiously creeping through the undergrowth, they were hacking and stomping their way through the brambles, cursing when they got scratched and making a right racket. There were no paths on this side of the pond. The land was as thorny and overgrown as the forest around Sleeping Beauty's castle.

They believe they're alone in the wood, Twitch thought, smiling to himself as he glimpsed the glow of their torch. If the Drakes thought the Twitchers had gone home with their tails between their legs, they were about to get a horrible shock. He pulled his camera out of the neck of his coat and spent a minute finding the spoonbill nest through the viewer. He saw the white bodies of the two sleeping birds, side by side, in their nest. Their feathers glowed in the moonlight like angels' wings.

"It must be here somewhere!" Evelyn took the torch from Merle and shone it along the water's edge, coming closer to Twitch's tree. They were about ten metres from the nest now. Jack is right, Twitch thought. She is more agile and sprightly than her cheery, waddling, daytime persona.

"Spoonbills nest in all manner of places," Merle said. "The nest could be in the reeds or even up a tree."

"This is why I like to scope out the nests in daylight," Evelyn grumbled. "It's almost impossible at night."

She was directly under Twitch now. He held his breath and gripped the log tightly as his blood pounded in his ears.

"No risk, no reward." Merle came to stand beside her. "This will be a new species of egg for our collection, darling." He stroked his hand down her back. "Think of how beautiful it will look in our waders' drawer."

Twitch's stomach churned to hear them talk.

"Umph!" Merle grunted, as suddenly a fat ball came out of nowhere and hit him square in the chest. "What the hell was that?" He spun around violently, shoving his wife to the side. Evelyn turned, looking as if she were about to shout at him, when a fat ball hit her on the back of the head, knocking her into him.

"Aargh!" she screeched as she grabbed Merle by the shoulders.

Feeling a squiggle of glee, Twitch glanced across

the pond, trying to spot Jack and Ava's boat, but it was hidden by the bulrushes.

"Who's there?" Merle shouted angrily, stomping towards the water, flashing his torch at the rushes. A hail of fat balls came out of the skies, pelting the pair of them. Merle staggered sideways and Evelyn ducked, shrieking as she covered her head with her arms. Twitch grinned as the man came in line with his branch; Twitch twisted and hurled the log away from him. It flew back, then dropped down so the rope pulled taut, swinging the log forward at speed. It hit Merle right on the bottom and sent the man hurtling forwards, face first into the pond.

"Just like playing skittles," Twitch muttered, as he speedily drew the rope back in, hand over hand, until he had the log back on his lap.

"What is happening?" Merle roared. As he emerged from the water, a fat ball hit him between the eyes.

A cloud that had been cloaking the moon moved on. Moonlight reflected off the surface of the pond, betraying the location of Jack and Ava's boat. Evelyn spotted them and jumped up. "There!" she cried, holding up her walking stick, twisting the silver duck's head and withdrawing a long-bladed silver knife. "It's those horrid kids!" She strode forward, assertive and fearless.

Twitch's throat went dry at the sight of the knife and his heart fluttered with fear for Ava and Jack.

Merle's smile was murderous. He wasn't afraid of children. He splashed towards them. "I'm going to drown you!" he bellowed.

"Get them, Merle," Evelyn shrieked, brandishing her knife from the shore.

A torrent of fat balls flew at him, but Merle batted them away, intent on getting to the boat. Twitch saw Jack rowing frantically as Ava threw the fat balls.

I have to help them, Twitch thought, turning and throwing the log out again, spinning back to see if it hit the mark. It missed, whistling by Evelyn's face. She pivoted to see who had thrown it at her and, as she did, it swung back, knocking the knife from her hand. Taking a breath, Twitch grabbed on to the second rope and jumped, swinging and twisting, holding his feet out in front of him. There was a crack as his boots connected with Evelyn's back and a splash as she flew into the water. He let go of the rope, falling to the ground, and grabbed the burgundy hat that had flown off her head. He tossed it up into the tree where it caught on a branch.

"Why you little…" Evelyn crawled from the black water with a face like a gargoyle. She grabbed her knife and rose up in front of Twitch, looking as if she were prepared to commit murder.

Twitch's reply stuck in his throat as his heart drilled through his ribs. He glanced at Merle, who had grabbed the prow of the boat and was roaring as he rocked it. Ava was desperately shining her torch into his face, trying to blind him. Jack kicked at the man's hands as he attempted to pitch them into the water. Twitch saw Jack lift an oar and bring it down on Merle's head.

"You," Evelyn said, as she came towards Twitch, "should be in jail!"

"I'm innocent," Twitch growled, taking a step back, his eyes fixed on her knife.

"You'll soon be dead." Her eyebrows lifted as she gave him a horrible smile.

"You wouldn't," Twitch said, taking another step away and letting out a squeak of fear as he found his back against a tree trunk. "That's murder!"

"Oh, I enjoy a bit of killing," Evelyn whispered. "I thought you knew that about me. Taking a life is power, you see. That's what I feel when I look at my thousands of eggshells. Power!"

"You're destroying nature!" Twitch shouted at her, feelings of terror locking his muscles so that he couldn't move, couldn't think, couldn't take his eyes off her knife!

"Nature is life and death, boy. Survival of the fittest. Kill or be killed."

"*TWITCH!*" came Jack's cry.

Over Evelyn Drake's shoulder Twitch saw two wet figures, Jack and Ava, scrambling up the bank. Evelyn turned her head, just as Jack ran at her, whacking the knife out of her hand with an oar. Ava pivoted and kicked at the back of her knees, and she crumbled to the ground.

Suddenly, the landscape blazed white as floodlights lit up the pond. It was as if the sun had shot back up into the sky and the night was banished. Twitch had to half-close his eyes against the brightness.

"This is the police!" came Inspector Khan's voice through a megaphone. "Stay exactly where you are. We have you surrounded. You are under arrest."

"Are you all right?" Jack was at Twitch's side, looking worried.

"I'm OK." He nodded.

"Do you think she means us too?" Ava asked.

"Mr Merle Drake, Mrs Evelyn Drake, I am arresting you for the attempted murder of three minors. You are also being charged with stealing birds' eggs and amassing an illegal collection."

"*No!*" Evelyn Drake shrieked.

"You do not have to say anything," Inspector Khan continued. "But, it may harm your defence if you do not mention when questioned something which you later rely on in court. Anything you do say may be given in evidence."

All at once there were police officers everywhere. Twitch, Jack and Ava were wrapped in blankets and the Drakes were handcuffed. Twitch was shivering but he felt euphoric. He looked out over Aves Wood, imagining all the sleeping birds hidden in their nests, safe now. He grinned at Jack. "We did it!"

"I'm just glad we're not dead," Ava said.

"Twitch! Jack!" Terry and Ozuru came crashing through the trees towards them. "Are you OK?" To his surprise, behind them followed a concerned looking Jed Butler with Constable Greenwood.

"Jed was at his tent," Terry gabbled. "He was going to come and protect the spoonbills. He thought you might try and steal their eggs!"

"He caught us," Ozuru added sheepishly.

"We told him everything," Terry butted in. "He drove us to the police station. We were there when Tara rang to report the Drakes!" He was buzzing with excitement. "I can't believe it was them!"

"Evening, Merle, Evelyn," Jed greeted the glowering

pair with a furious look. "Constable, that is the woman who told me she saw Corvus Featherstone up at the pike, below the peregrine falcon nest, last Thursday night. She told me she didn't want to go to the police and report it herself because her son had been in trouble with the law and police stations upset her. Having been in trouble with the law myself, I empathized and volunteered to report him for her. I must confess to relaying her testimony as my own, but I only did so because it is my life's work to protect birds. I saw him running away from the hill when the police were investigating the nest and thought he looked frightened and guilty. Later, when I met Corvus by the canal, I noted his interest in birds' eggs. He was talking about finding a bullfinch's nest. I mistakenly thought he intended to steal the eggs inside. I shared my concerns with Mrs Drake. She encouraged me to make a second report." He bowed his head but looked Twitch in the eyes. "I would like to apologize to you, Corvus. I know what you must've been through."

"I owe you the same apology," Twitch said, with a shy smile. "I was positive it was you who was stealing the eggs."

"Understandable." Jed looked ashamed.

"I do have one question," Twitch said. "Was it you who found my binoculars?"

Jed shook his head and they both looked at the Drakes. Evelyn Drake smiled but said nothing.

"Inspector Khan," said an officer behind Constable Greenwood. "There are two girls beside the Drakes' car. They instructed our officers to open the boot and look inside Mr Drake's fishing tackle box. Officer Cooper just radioed in. She says that, beneath the maggots and worms, there are compartments full of unblown birds' eggs, including the missing three from the peregrine falcons' nest."

Everyone turned to look at the Drakes.

"Take them away," Inspector Khan ordered, and two officers marched the sopping wet Merle and Evelyn away from the pond.

"Inspector Khan." Twitch pointed up to Evelyn's burgundy hat, which was hanging from a branch above them. "That is an important piece of evidence. The hat has a false bottom. That's where she puts the eggs. You'll find three fake spoonbill eggs in there that she attempted to steal from a fake nest we set up as a trap. The eggs you found in the hide, she transported under her hat and planted in Tara's Tupperware."

"Er, thank you," Inspector Khan replied, staring up into the branches. "Look, I admit we were wrong to charge you. I would like to formally apologize. I was just trying to do my job. First thing tomorrow morning, all charges will be dropped."

"YES!" Jack punched the air.

"Now, let's get you children home," said Constable Greenwood.

"Thanks, but first," Twitch said, "can you get the floodlights turned off and tell everyone to be quiet. You're disturbing the birds."

34
THE EGG HUNT

Twitch was so happy he felt his skin might sprout feathers. The trees were bustling with birds and the spring winds had cleared the clouds from the sky. The sun was warm on his cheeks. When Jack's mum answered the door, it took all his self-control not to push past her and run into the house.

"Happy Easter, Maggie," his mum said, handing Jack's mum a plate of chocolate brownies she'd baked for the party.

"Oh, Iris, these look delicious! Go on, Twitch, Jack is out the back. The weather is perfect for an egg hunt."

Twitch rushed through to the kitchen where Dr Sawa was leaning against the breakfast bar talking to Jack's dad.

"Jack tells me the police discovered an enormous egg collection at the Drakes' home. Thousands upon thousands of eggs. Can you imagine?" Jack's dad was saying.

"What will happen to them?" Dr Sawa asked. "Will they be destroyed?"

"Not sure. It looks like the Drakes will be serving a prison sentence. There are a number of charges against them. The evidence being what it is, they'll have no choice but to plead guilty."

Through the open patio doors, Twitch saw the others in the back garden. "Jack! Jack! You'll never guess what!"

"Twitch!" Jack greeted him. "We've been waiting for you."

"The swallows are here!" Twitch cried, jigging with delight. "They arrived yesterday. The male has been singing up a storm and perching on my window ledge fanning his tail all morning!"

Jack whooped. "Now it's really spring!"

Everyone was gathered around the patio table. Twitch saw that Ava had finally got to wear her purple tracksuit. Vernon, Pam and Clem were there too. Twitch thought Terry might be annoyed by his nemesis being invited, but he seemed unusually happy and was grinning at everyone.

"We've got one more guest to arrive and then we can begin the egg hunt," Jack told him.

"I'm going to get a cola," Terry said. "Does anyone want one?"

"I do," Pam said.

"Does anyone except Pam want one?" Terry asked, turning his back to her.

"I'll have one," Ozuru said.

Terry darted into the kitchen and came out clutching two bottles. "Hey, Clem, film this." He handed one bottle to Ozuru then stood right next to Pam. Clem turned the camera on him as he opened the bottle with a crack and a fizz. "Mmm, delicious cola," Terry said, grinning maddeningly at Pam, waving the bottle in front of her face. Then he lifted the bottle to take a sip.

"Thanks," Pam said, snatching it out of his hand and helping herself to a big swig. Her face contorted in sudden shock, then revulsion. There was an explosion of spray as she spat cola all over Clem and the camera. "Urgh! Oh my god! What is that?" She threw the bottle away, doubling over and spitting what was left in her mouth onto the pavement. "Urgh! What did you put in there? It's gross!"

"What did you do that for?" Clem wailed, looking down at the brown stains all over his white T-shirt. "My mum's going to kill me!"

"Wham! Bam!" crowed Terry. "How do *you* like being pranked, Pam?"

Twitch laughed as Terry danced around in front of Pam, chanting, "You just drank fizzy soy sauce! You drank fizzy soy sauce!"

Pam snatched up the half-empty bottle from the ground and chased after Terry, grabbing his arm and whirling him, trying to splash him with the drink.

"You know what those two remind me of?" Jack said with a chuckle. "That pair of peregrine falcons."

The back door opened, and Mr Bettany came into the garden, followed by a bashful Pippa, who was hanging back behind her grandad.

"Pippa!" Jack called out. "Come and join us; we're about to have an egg hunt."

Twitch noticed she was nervously pulling at the hem of her jumper as Mr Bettany coaxed her forward.

Tippi ran up to her and linked her arm through Pippa's. "Hi, I'm Tippi."

"Um, hi." Pippa blushed furiously.

"Can I ask her, Jack?" Tippi said.

"Ask her what?" Twitch looked at Jack, who winked at him.

"Pippa, we've got something very important to ask you," Jack told her.

Pippa looked terrified.

"We'd like to invite you to become an honorary member of the Twitchers," Tara said softly.

"What?" Pippa was shocked.

"Yes," Tippi said, doing a merry dance beside her. "We need more girls."

"Honestly, being an honorary Twitcher is the way to go," Pam told her. "You don't have to hang out in their mud hut but you get to do the exciting stuff."

Vernon nodded.

"But…" Pippa turned to Twitch. "I got you in trouble, and … and…" Her lip trembled. "I thought you wanted me to come here so you could shout at me."

"You don't really think I'm that mean!" Twitch exclaimed.

"No…" She glanced at Jack.

Ava laughed.

"Pippa, I'd love you to be one of the Twitchers," Twitch said, "but it wasn't my idea to invite you to join."

"Nope. That was mean old me," Jack said, grinning. "Although Tippi is the one who pointed out you were only trying to protect your grandad. Anyway. We all voted on it. It was unanimous. We want you to join."

"I didn't get a vote!" Twitch said.

"We all knew you would vote yes," Ava pointed out.

Twitch grinned. "I would have."

"So, what do you say?" Terry asked Pippa. "Want to become a Twitcher?"

"Oh, yes, please!" Pippa glanced at her grandad, who gave her a thumbs up.

"Hooray," Tippi shouted. "I can teach you our oath."

"Oh, I already know it," Pippa told her with a shy smile.

"Listen," Jack said to the group. "My mum has been hiding eggs all morning. Can you act like you're really excited when you find them? Give a cheer or a whoop, that kind of thing?"

"What do you mean, act?" Vernon said. "Finding eggs is brilliant. I'm going to find more eggs than any of you."

"Oh, yeah?" Terry stuck out his chin. "You won't get more than me. I'd put a tenner on it."

"You're on!" Vernon punched his fist into his palm.

"Oooh, let's make this spicy," Pam said. "Every egg you find, no matter how big or small, you have to immediately unwrap and stuff in your mouth. You aren't allowed to pick up a second egg until you've swallowed the first. Most eggs eaten, wins."

Terry and Vernon eyed each other up and nodded.

"You don't know who you're going up against," Vernon said, puffing out his chest.

"Yeah? Well, I'm the youngest of seven. You have no idea how fast I can eat chocolate." Terry smacked his lips. "I've practised for this my whole life."

They each grabbed a basket from the pile laid on the patio table. Jack shouted "GO", and everyone ran around plucking gold, red, blue and green shiny eggs from their hiding places, shrieking with laughter as Vernon and Terry stuffed chocolate into their mouths at a furious rate.

"Twitch." Mr Bettany waved him over. "Constable Greenwood stopped by the newsagent's this morning. I think he was hoping to catch you at the end of your newspaper round. I said I'd be seeing you and he asked if I could give you these." From his bag he withdrew Twitch's grandad's binoculars.

"Oh! Thank you." Twitch hugged them to his chest and smiled at his mum. She was the only person who really understood how precious they were to him. He pulled the strap over his head, feeling more like himself the moment the weight of the field glasses pressed against his chest.

"He also said to pass on his apologies, but that he'd give them to you in person next time he saw you. He wanted you to know he's spoken to the Aves Wood Wildlife Committee and you're welcome in the nature reserve."

"You got them back!" Jack cried, seeing the binoculars around his neck.

"Yes!" Twitch waggled them at him. "And I've got an Easter gift for you." From his pocket he drew one of Peter Landrow's fake spoonbill eggs and handed it to Jack. "As a souvenir of our adventures."

"Wow. Thank you. This is going to be the best spring!" Jack told him happily, as they sat down to eat their chocolate.

"Yes." Twitch grinned. "Because we're going to have spoonbill chicks to watch."

ACKNOWLEDGEMENTS

Declining bird populations are a very real problem. I recently wrote an essay on the starling for a book called *Into the Red* produced by the British Trust for Ornithology, and was shocked to discover that this once ubiquitous bird is under threat. You can read about mine and other contributions to this important bird book here: bto.org/community/blog/making-red.

I was inspired to write this story by an unsettling wildlife documentary called *Poached!*, directed by Timothy Wheeler, about the boyhood hobby of egg collecting becoming a destructive obsession.

The egg artist in this story is based on Peter Rowland, who creates beautiful replicas for museums and galleries. I have one of his blackbird eggs. You can see his work here: originalreplicabirdseggs.co.uk.

If you've read *Twitch* or *Spark*, you'll know that Aves Wood is based on a real place called Cromwell Bottom Nature Reserve. If you find yourself in the Calder Valley, I recommend stopping by and paying it a visit.

It is a beautiful place. You can find out more about it here: cromwellbottomlnr.co.uk.

This book was written at a time when my life was in extreme flux. The world was opening up after the pandemic. I moved house twice in six months, and rented an office to keep writing. The number of projects I was working on was absurd. I'm grateful to Walker Books for their patience and understanding at this truly tricky time. In particular, I must thank Megan Middleton, Jenny Bish and Denise Johnstone-Burt, as well as Kirsten, Ben, Ed and everyone at Walker Books who has played a part in making this book.

Paddy Donnelly is responsible for all The Twitchers stunning cover art. I think *Clutch* could be my favourite. Thank you, Paddy. I feel very lucky to have you creating the covers for these books.

My family inspire, challenge, support and depend on me to be good at what I do, which is a huge driver in my life. Thank you, Arthur, Sebastian and my amazing manager and husband, Sam Harmsworth-Sparling.

My agent Kirsty McLachlan is a legend, a monolith, a giant, my shield bearer, and my friend. Thank you, Kirsty. I know all that you do for me and am grateful.

To all you bird-lovers out there, these adventures

are for you. I hope you enjoy reading them as much as I enjoy writing them, and I'd like to encourage you to use the word "oology" as often as you can. It's very satisfying.

Discover the Twitchers' first mystery adventure!

Twitch has three pet chickens, four pigeons, swallows nesting in his bedroom and a passion for birdwatching. On the first day of the summer holidays, he arrives at his secret hide to find police everywhere. A convicted robber has broken out of prison and is hiding in Aves Wood. Can Twitch use his talents for birdwatching in the hunt for the dangerous prisoner and find the missing loot?

WINNER OF THE CRIMEFEST AWARD FOR BEST CRIME NOVEL FOR CHILDREN 2021

WINNER OF THE SAINSBURY'S CHILDREN'S BOOK AWARDS 2021

A thrilling crime
for the Twitchers to solve!

When Jack rescues a wounded cat, he quickly suspects foul play.
Could there be a wildlife criminal on the loose in Briddvale?
Jack rushes to investigate, determined to catch the culprit, only
to stumble into a deepening mystery and a sinister criminal plot.
Can Jack and the Twitchers stop the villains before it's too late?

"A skilfully crafted mystery adventure.
A clarion call for environmentalists everywhere."

ROB BIDDULPH, *LOVEREADING4KIDS*

M. G. LEONARD is an award-winning, bestselling writer of children's books, as well as a member of Authors4Oceans. Her books are sold in 40 countries, and there is currently a TV series in development based on her Beetle Boy series. Her first picture book, *The Tale of a Toothbrush*, is out now. She is also co-author of the critically acclaimed Adventures on Trains series, and the author of The Twitchers, a mystery adventure series starring a group of birdwatching detectives. Before becoming a writer, M. G. Leonard worked as a digital media producer for the National Theatre, The Royal Opera House and Shakespeare's Globe. She lives by the sea with her husband, two sons and pet beetles.

#TheTwitchers
@WalkerBooksUK
@MGLnrd